Stay
WILD

NEW YORK TIMES BESTSELLING AUTHOR

KAYLEE RYAN

Cover Design: Book Cover Boutique
Cover Photography: Sara Eirew
Editing: Hot Tree Editing
Proofreading: Deaton Author Services. Editing 4 Indies,
Jo Thompson, Jess Hodge
Paperback Formatting: Integrity Formatting

WWW.KAYLEERYAN.COM

Stay
WILD

NEW YORK TIMES BESTSELLING AUTHOR
KAYLEE RYAN

WWW.KAYLEERYAN.COM

Stay
WILD

NEW YORK TIMES BESTSELLING AUTHOR
KAYLEE RYAN

Chapter 1

ARCHER

"OFF LIMITS," I MUTTER UNDER my breath. My brothers think they're funny. Unless it's his wife, Brooks has no say so, and I'm about to prove it as I stalk toward the redheaded beauty. He thinks because she's here working for Palmer, that he can make the rules. He didn't give a fuck about the rules when he was sneaking around with Palmer behind everyone's back. He doesn't get to try and make rules and enforce them now. I know he's doing it to get under my skin, and it worked.

I've been watching her all day. She's smiled and laughed with every member of my family. Every member but me. I'm not the standout among my siblings. I'm the guy who keeps the twins in line when I can and can still hold a conversation and drink a cold beer with our older brothers. I don't date often, and it's been far too long since I've been inside a woman.

Maybe that's about to change.

Her long red hair hangs over her shoulder. The locks look like silk, and my fingers twitch to reach out and touch them. She's wearing a floral top that's loose but does nothing to hide her figure since it's a sheer material. She's got a white tank top beneath it and is wearing white dress pants and black fuck-me heels. I've watched her bend and twist all day to get just the right angle for the photo she was taking. If you'd told me that watching a photographer was a turn-on, I would have called you an idiot, unless you're my brother Brooks who's married to one. I don't think he got to see her in action. If he had, he would have dropped to one knee a hell of a lot sooner than he did. I've never spoken a word to the redheaded beauty, and the thought has crossed my mind.

"You look like you could use a drink," I say once I'm standing in front of her.

She lowers her camera and smiles. It's a bright, blinding smile that makes her green eyes sparkle and lights up the entire fucking room. "Thank you, but I'm working."

"I'm sure my sister-in-law won't mind." I glance around the room, looking for Palmer. She's talking to Ramsey and not paying a bit of attention to us. I turn back to her, not able to look away for long.

"Oh, you're another brother." She laughs. "I've lost track of how many of you I've met today."

"One of nine," I tell her.

"Your momma... she's a rockstar. Sweet as pie too." She chuckles.

"I agree on both counts." I shove my hands inside my pants pockets because all I want to do is reach out and touch those luscious red locks and see if they're as soft as they appear. "I'm Archer." I should offer her my hand to shake, but this urge to pull her into me is too strong. It's best to avoid contact at the moment. There are too many witnesses around, and the things I've been thinking about doing to this beautiful woman all day are still at the forefront of my mind.

"Nice to meet you, Archer. I'm Scarlett." Her voice is raspy and sexy as fuck.

"So, a drink?" I'm trying not to sound desperate to spend time with her, but I'm failing. I don't know that I've ever seen a woman more beautiful.

"I don't think I should. I'm working, and this is sort of my interview." She lifts her camera and gives it a little shake in her hand.

I open my mouth to say, what... I'm not sure. I'm stopped by a hand on my arm. When I look over, I see who saved me from making a fool of myself. "Hey, you two." My sister-in-law Palmer appears beside us. "Scarlett, you've been amazing. Thank you for being here to help. You're off the hook for the rest of the night. Meet me at the studio around nine on Monday. We'll work through your paperwork and get you on the schedule."

"What?" Scarlett's smile is wider than before, which I didn't think was possible. "Seriously?" She moves forward and pulls Palmer into a hug. "Thank you so much, Palmer. I'm so excited to get to work with you."

"Thank you for putting up with my interview idea."

"Wait. You haven't seen any of my images from today." Scarlett punches some buttons on her screen and turns it so that Palmer can see.

Palmer waves her off. "Oh, it was never your quality of work I was questioning. You've got mad skills with your camera. I just needed someone like me who can talk to anyone and make their subject feel at ease. I wanted to see you in action, and from what I've witnessed today, you're going to be a perfect fit for Captured Moments. I think you and I are going to get along just fine."

"Thank you." Scarlett nods and offers Palmer another bright smile.

"Now, put that camera away and join the party. Archer, why don't you grab her a drink?" Palmer winks at me before turning and walking away.

I make a mental note to offer to babysit Remi anytime she wants. Palmer just moved into the favorite sister-in-law spot. Well, that's not actually true. I love all of my brothers' wives and my sisters by marriage. My brothers are lucky assholes to find the ladies that they have.

"What's your poison?" I ask.

"I'm a vodka and Mountain Dew kind of girl," she says with a chuckle. "VooDew." She winks.

"Interesting combination."

"Hey." She mock glares at me. "Don't knock it until you've tried it."

"I'll take your word for it. I'll stick to beer." I motion for her to lead the way to the bar, and she grins before heading that way. I follow along behind her, watching as her ass sways in those dress pants she's wearing. They're not so tight that they're indecent, but you can tell that what lies beneath is something you want to sink

4 | KAYLEE RYAN

your teeth into. Okay, maybe that's just me, but yeah, I could see myself taking a bite of that ass.

"Are you staring at my ass?" Scarlett calls me out.

I think about lying for about two seconds before I nod. "Yep."

"It's nice, right?" She grins and turns back around, taking the final few steps to reach the bar.

My steps falter. That was not at all the response I was expecting. By the time I'm sliding up to the bar next to her, she's ordered both of us a drink. "Thanks," I tell the bartender, raising my drink to Scarlett's for a toast.

"Oh, what are we toasting?" she asks, her drink raised in the air but not yet close enough to tap against mine.

"True love," I say, nodding toward my brother and his bride.

Scarlett tilts her head to the side. "You believe?"

I shrug. "It's kind of hard not to in my family. My parents are still madly in love with one another, and as one of nine brothers who has watched five of my brothers declare their undying love for the ladies in their lives, I'd be crazy not to." I take a sip of my drink. "What about you?"

"Meh, I think it exists, but I'm not sure it's for everyone."

"Never been in love, huh?" I ask.

"Nope. What about you?"

"Nah. I've dated, but there hasn't been anyone who I felt I had to have more of."

"That's an interesting way to put it."

"I'm just telling it like it is. That's the point of dating, right? You spend time together. You get to know each other on an intimate and emotional level. You have to want to get to know that person that way, and so far, no one has made me want that."

"But she's out there, right?" She offers me a smile that lights up this entire fucking room.

"Yeah," I agree. "I'm certain she's out there."

Scarlett shakes her head, sipping her own drink. "It's refreshing," she says after a few moments of taking in the crowd while my eyes are glued to her.

"Vodka and Mountain Dew?" I ask.

"This big, loving family." She pulls her gaze from my family and turns it on me. "To be standing next to a man who is so obviously sexy... that is open and honest about his thoughts on relationships."

"Nothing to hide." Bringing my glass to my lips, I take a long pull to hide my grin. She thinks I'm sexy.

"What you see is what you get, huh?"

"I guess you could say that."

She points her index finger at me. "That, too, is refreshing."

"What about you?" I lean my elbow on the bar. The action brings us a little closer, and her floral scent wraps around me.

Intoxicating.

"Never been in love," she replies instantly. "Not sure I'm made for being tied down, if I'm being honest."

"Yeah?"

She nods. "I want to be a travel photographer. There are so many amazing places to visit in the world. That's hard to do when you have a husband and kids at home."

"What about your family?"

"We're not close. Not really. I was adopted. My adoptive dad passed away when I was in middle school, and my adoptive mom the year after I graduated high school. They didn't have a lot of family, and no other kids, so it's just me."

Lifting my hand to my chest, I rub that instant ache that appeared hearing her words. "I'm sorry for your loss." I don't know what else to say. I know my words mean dick. What I want to tell her is that she can be a part of our family. It's growing by the day, and I know for certain my parents, my brothers, and my sisters-in-law would welcome her into our loud, rambunctious family. We can share ours with her.

She smiles. It's soft, and I can see a sadness that I know she's trying to hide. She'd probably succeed had I not been studying her all damn day. "Thank you. It's the hand I was dealt."

"So, Willow River?"

"When my mom passed, I had to sell the house to pay for her medical bills. I packed up what I needed with my camera and started to travel. Nothing exotic. I spent a year in Nevada and another in Washington State. I've been taking freelance jobs, and I've been getting by." She takes a long pull from her glass. "I was looking late one night at job openings on this photography site I'm on, and I saw the ad for Captured Moments. I looked up the town, and it seemed like a good place to land for a while."

"So, we're just a stepping stone for you?" I pause. "Does Palmer know that?" It doesn't matter how bad I want her. I still need to look out for my family. Palmer's been talking about adding a photographer so she can spend more time with Remi for a long time. I'd hate for her to get settled and Scarlett up and leave her.

"Yes, and before you go all Hulk on me." She must see the confusion written on my face. "Your hand fisted up." She nods to where my hand is sure enough in a fist hanging at my side. "And you bulked up. I mean, why do you need all of those muscles anyway?"

I'm not sure if she expects an answer, but I'm not giving her one. Instead, I stare her down, waiting for her to answer mine.

"Palmer knows. I was upfront with her that my time here is limited. I agreed that I would sign on for a year, and then we could go from there."

I feel my shoulders relax at her confession. Scarlett reaches out and places her hand on my bicep. I follow the movement with my eyes and try to mask what I feel from her touching me, even through my dress shirt.

"Sorry." She grins. "I just had to make sure they were real. I mean, I thought maybe you might have blow-up biceps under there or something."

I don't even try to hide my laughter. "I'm not even sure how to respond to that."

"No need. I felt the proof." She winks, and her green eyes sparkle. "Do you eat a lot of spinach?" she asks, barely containing her laughter.

"Umm, does it count if it's the dip my mom makes?"

She nods. "Sure thing, Popeye."

A laugh falls from my lips. "Not much of a sailor."

"Well, it was either Popeye or arm porn guy. I figured I should clean it up for the kiddos."

I choke on my drink. "Arm porn?"

"Come on now, Archer. You can't tell me you don't know that that"—she points at my biceps—"is referred to as arm porn."

"Never. Not in my entire life have I heard that."

"What? How is that possible when you look like you? What is wrong with the women in this town?" Scarlett shakes her head as if my not knowing about this crazy arm porn phenomenon she speaks of is just unheard of. I take a sip of my beer to hide my amusement. She's seriously irritated or baffled, I guess is a better way to explain her current mood, that I've never heard of it before now.

"Alyssa!" Scarlett reaches out and grabs my sister-in-law's wrist. "Help me out here."

"What's up?" Alyssa gives Scarlett a kind smile.

"You two know each other?" I ask.

"Oh, yeah, we met earlier." Scarlett waves her hand in the air.

I know she's talked to everyone, but to remember their names and to talk as if they're old friends is surprising. Then again, there's nothing about the beautiful Scarlett that says she is like anyone I've ever met. This one is a firecracker, for sure.

"Anyway, this guy"—Scarlett points at me—"has never heard of arm porn."

"Really?" Alyssa asks. "How is that possible? I mean, all nine of you are perfect examples."

"Perfect examples of what?" Sterling asks as he joins us, wrapping his arms around his wife from behind.

"Arm porn."

"Arm what now?" he asks.

Scarlett and Alyssa fall into a fit of laughter. "Arm porn." Alyssa turns in his arms and squeezes his biceps. "This," she tells him.

"Why is that turning me on?" Sterling asks with a glint in his eyes.

"On that note." I finish off my beer and set the empty on the table. I hold my hand out for Scarlett. "You're new in town, but let me help you out here. My brothers, when it comes to their wives, and our dad, too, they don't care who is around." I point to my brother, who is now lip-locked with his wife. "Save me. Dance with me." I jut out my bottom lip in a pout, and Scarlett tosses her head back in laughter.

"I don't want your life on my conscience." Scarlett winks. She places her hand in mine. "Show me what you've got, Popeye." Grasping her hand, I lead her to the dance floor, spinning her around and into my arms. "Oh, I see how it is. You got moves." She shimmies her hips against mine.

"Just putting all the arm porn to good use," I banter back.

Scarlett nods. "Very good point. I mean, if you got it, flaunt it, right?"

I chuckle and lower my head so my lips are next to her ear. "You're a firecracker."

She smiles up at me. Her green eyes are sparkling. "Less talking, more dancing. I need to see what these babies can do." She squeezes my biceps before sliding her arms around my neck.

"Yes, ma'am." I pull her close as we sway to the beat. My gaze skims the room as I watch my brothers with their wives, my parents, our nieces, and nephews. The Kincaid brood really is growing.

One song bleeds into another, and Scarlett and I continue to sway back and forth. Her hands are now in my hair, and my hands are resting on the small of her back, holding her close. When the beat changes and the steady strum of bass flows from the speakers, I look down to see Scarlett smirking at me.

"Did you eat your spinach today?" she asks.

"Nope."

"Damn, I hope you can keep up." She slides one long slender leg between my own and straddles my knee before she starts to bump and grind.

My cock instantly hardens. I don't think about my family that I'm sure is watching our every move. I don't think about how I just met this girl, and she's lit my entire body on fire. I let everything but Scarlett fall away.

I grip her hips as I help guide her. Her mouth falls open as desire pools in those emerald-green eyes.

I want her.

The look in her gaze tells me that she wants me too. I mentally calculate how much longer until we can slip away unnoticed.

Sterling has his wife pressed tightly to his chest as they stand in the center of the dance floor, lips locked. Everyone around them is moving and gyrating to the beat, but those two, the newly married couple, are lost in their own little world. I've never felt love like that, but as I stare down at the sexy firecracker that's grinding her pussy on my thigh, I get the appeal.

I get bored easily. However, something tells me that there will never be a boring moment in the presence of the beautiful Scarlett.

Chapter 2

SCARLETT

I DON'T KNOW WHAT THEY'RE feeding these men here in Willow River, but damn! It should be illegal for one family to have all the good genes. Nine brothers, all fine as hell. Although, if I'm being honest, the sexiest Kincaid brother is mine. Well, not mine, but you know what I mean. For this moment, while we're out here on the dance floor, and I'm grinding myself on his thigh, I'm considering him mine.

I have a feeling that my time here in Willow River is going to be something that I'll always remember. I mean, arm porn for days. I saw him as soon as I arrived, but I avoided him. Well, kind of avoided him. I told myself I was just focused on my job. I knew the hottie Popeye arms would distract me.

Arm. Porn.

It deserves repeating.

His big, strong hand slides up my back and cups the back of my neck while the other remains splayed on the small of my back, holding me close. So close, in fact, I'm not exactly sure where he ends and I begin.

I don't hate it.

"So sexy," he rumbles in his deep, whispered voice.

This man thinks I'm sexy? Has he looked in the mirror? I mean, yeah, I know that I'm pretty. So many men seem to have a redhead fantasy, but this man, Archer Kincaid, he's on another level.

He's well over my five foot six inches. I'd say he's at least six two or three. His dark hair is shorter on the sides and longer on the top. Not something I would have considered sexy, but this beast of a man pulls it off flawlessly. He's wearing a long-sleeve button-up, and it's stretched over his biceps. I don't need to see him naked to have an idea of what he's hiding underneath.

And his legs. Strong. Thick. Powerful. Trust me on this one. I'm currently grinding up on him like a cat in heat, and I couldn't give a single fuck what anyone thinks. I should. My new boss is here— she's his family—but I'm so lost in this man that consequences be damned. I'm in the moment.

My mom always told me I had a wild spirit. I hear her voice constantly saying those words—she's here with me now—but it's not enough to stop me. Not when I am the center of Archer's attention.

I want his attention.

I want his eyes on me.

I want to grind on him for as long as he'll let me.

I want him.

"What do you want, Firecracker?" he asks as though reading my mind. He rests his forehead against mine, and the act is intimate, which lights my desire for him to where the flames are burning so high, I'm not sure we'll ever be able to extinguish them.

"You," I whisper, but he hears me. His intake of breath tells me he does. It could also be the way his hand on the small of my back grips the back of my shirt. I imagine that being in my hair and heat pools between my thighs.

Correction. More heat pools between my thighs. The panties I put on this morning are ruined. Soaked. So much so that I wouldn't be surprised if the evidence were not all over his thigh. Thankfully he's wearing black dress pants.

He leans in close, his lips a breath from mine. He's going to kiss me. I want him to kiss me. He hovers there, just out of reach. I could close the distance, erase the small gap between his lips and mine, but he needs to work for it. He leans in a little closer, and instead of the kiss I was anticipating, he speaks.

"You want to get out of here?" His hot breath floats across my skin, and I try not to let my disappointment of not getting a kiss show.

"Yes." There is zero hesitation in my reply. One-night stands are not something that I indulge in often. In fact, it's been far too long since I've been with anyone. However, I've always been one to follow my gut, and my gut tells me that not only is Archer Kincaid a good guy, but that he knows his way around a woman's body.

I shiver at the thought.

"Did you drive here?"

"I did."

"We can leave it here. I'll bring you back tomorrow."

"I'd rather drive to yours if that's okay. I have almost everything I own in my car. I'm staying at a hotel for now. I was waiting to see if I got the job before I looked for something more permanent."

He stands to his full height and nods. "Fine. Where's your stuff?"

"In the back room." I nod toward the door that leads to the kitchen area.

"I need to say goodbye to my family. Meet me at the back door?"

"Okay."

"Don't go out without me. It's late and dark out."

"I've been taking care of myself for a long time," I tell him.

He nods. "That might be true, but tonight, you're going home with me. You're going to be in my bed, coming on my tongue, my hands, and my cock. Tonight, you let me look out for you."

I open my mouth to argue but quickly close it. I don't want to argue. One night of letting someone else take on the responsibility, make the choices, and worry about me, sounds almost too good to be true. It's been a long time since I've been with a man. It's been even longer since I've had someone who wanted to look out for me.

Sure, there's my best friend, Natasha, but she's married and settled down in Idaho, my home state. She and I talk all the time, and we video chat, but she's not here. She worries, but it's hard to do much else living in a different state.

"Okay."

Archer removes the hand that was holding me by the back of my neck and traces his knuckle over my cheek. "So pretty and so agreeable."

"It's the arm porn," I blurt.

He tosses his head back and laughs. It's a deep, rich sound that wraps around me like a warm winter blanket. Not just any blanket. One that's been recently laundered and fresh out of the dryer. It's nice and warm and soothing.

"Ten minutes."

"You're going to say goodbye to all of these people in ten minutes?" I raise a questioning brow.

"Yes. I have a good incentive." He winks, and I'm thankful he's holding on to me because the action causes my knees to go weak. He leans in and presses his lips to my forehead. "Nine minutes," he murmurs.

He releases me from his hold, turns, and walks away. I'm not ashamed to admit that I stand here for several long heartbeats and watch him go. He reaches his brother and his new wife, and I know that I need to get moving. I've had a few one-night stands. None of them have ever had me this worked up.

I spot Palmer in the corner, and my feet carry me in that direction.

"I'm going to head out," I tell her when I reach them. I offer my finger to her daughter, who smiles as she curls up into her daddy's chest.

"Be safe. Do you need a ride?" she asks.

"No. I only had one beer, and my car is here." I leave out the part where I tell her that pretty much my entire life in is my car, and I don't want to be too far away from it. I also leave out the fact that I'm going home with her brother-in-law. It's my personal time, so that shouldn't matter. In fact, it doesn't.

I want the job, but I want this night with Archer even more.

I've never felt this kind of instant connection.

"Well, thank you again for being here. I'll see you on Monday."

With a smile and a wave, I head toward the back room to gather my things and wait for Archer. When I make it to the back door, he's already there waiting on me. As if he's done it a thousand times before, he takes my camera bag from my shoulder and tosses it over his, then slides his arm around my waist and leads me out to the parking lot.

"Where are you parked?" he asks.

"There." I point to my ten-year-old Subaru Outback. "The white Subaru."

"It's as if the universe is trying to tell us that this is a good idea. That's me." He points to the big royal blue truck with a shiny chrome GMC emblem on the front.

He walks me to my car and waits for me to unlock the door. Once I'm settled behind the wheel, he leans in. "I'll see you at my place. I'll drive slow so that I don't lose you."

"Sounds like a plan." I reach out for my camera bag, but he steps out of my reach. "I can take that."

"Nah, this is my insurance." He winks, and the heat that pools between my thighs is embarrassing.

"You don't trust me?"

His eyes smolder under the streetlights. "It's more like I want you too much to risk it." With those parting words, he stands to his full height. My camera bag is still strung over his shoulder as he steps back to shut my car door. He taps on the roof three times before he walks to the driver's side of his truck and climbs inside.

My hands shake as I place them on the wheel. Archer flashes his lights and pulls his truck out of his spot. Slowly, I press the gas and follow behind him. All I can think about on the drive is the way his body felt close to mine on the dance floor. I squirm in my seat and huff out a breath.

"You're acting like a sex fiend," I mumble as I pull into a driveway behind Archer. He jumps out of his truck and is at my door, tugging it open before I have the chance to turn the engine off.

Archer doesn't say a word. He simply slides his arm around my waist and leads me inside. It's not until we're in his house and the lights are on that I realize my camera bag is once again sitting on his shoulder.

"Thanks for that." I point to the bag.

"I figured you wouldn't want it sitting outside in my truck all night." He places the bag on the kitchen counter.

"You would be correct."

"Would you like something to drink?"

"So formal," I tease, partially to torment him and partially to help calm my nerves. I don't know why I'm nervous. He's just a man. A very sexy man. One that I just met, yet here I am in his home with him all on my own. Luckily, I spent the entire day with his family, and I'm a good judge of character. My gut never steers me wrong, and my instincts tell me that Archer Kincaid is one of the good guys.

"Polite." He offers me a sexy grin. "My momma raised me right."

"You and your eight brothers."

"Yeah, and for a few years, my cousin Ramsey. She was there at the wedding tonight with her husband, Deacon."

I nod because I remember meeting her and asking if she was a sister, and she explained that she was a cousin and that her aunt and uncle took her in. She was an adult at the time but needed a safe place to land, and they gladly opened their home to her.

As I said, good people.

"A drink?" he asks again.

"No, thank you."

"So formal." He changes his voice to mimic my own.

I chuckle, but it quickly dies on my lips as he steps closer to me. He grips my hips and lifts me to the kitchen island, stepping between my thighs. I could say he pushed in, making room for himself, but I'd be lying. I opened for him. Ready and willing to be close to him.

As he braces his hands on the counter, his gaze locks with mine. "Your eyes. They're mesmerizing."

"I'm a sure thing, Popeye." I fist his shirt and tug him closer. He stands to his full height and pushes his hips forward, where his very hard cock presses against my core. We're both still fully clothed, and I can tell it's not just his arms that are huge. "But you have to promise me you won't fall in love with me. Feelings are messy, and I'm only here for a year."

"That might be true, but like I said, my momma raised me right. And I could say the same for you. No love. Just sex."

"Oh, so your momma taught you about seduction?" I wrap my arms around his neck, which brings him even closer.

"She taught me respect. I may want to fuck you, Scarlett, but I also respect you."

"You don't know me."

"I know that you're beautiful. I know that you have a passion for photography. I know that you lost your parents and that you're floating from state to state, from city to city. I know that you have a wild streak inside you that doesn't want to be tamed."

Damn. Okay, so he listens well. "And you have no plan to try and tame me?"

"I don't want to tame you." He leans in and trails kisses from my collarbone to my ear. "You still want this? You still want me?" His voice is deep and gravelly, and I don't think I've ever heard a voice sexier than his.

"Yes."

"At any time, if you change your mind, you tell me, and we stop."

"I'm not going to want you to stop." To prove to him that this is the case, I tilt my head to the side, giving him better access to nip at my throat.

"Wrap your legs around my waist, Firecracker."

I don't hesitate to do as he asks. I wrap my legs around his waist, locking at the ankles. "Now what are you going to do with me?" I tease. There's a glint of mischief and an abundance of need in his gaze.

"Ruin you for other men." He growls the words as he lifts me from the island, and we're moving. I hold on tight, burying my face in his neck and placing soft kisses against his skin. He grips my ass tighter, and his steps quicken as we make our way down a dark hallway. His boot thuds against the door as he kicks it open, and then I'm being gently tossed onto the bed, which makes me laugh.

The room is flooded with low lighting from the bedside lamp as Archer starts to unbutton his dress shirt.

"Oh, is this when the gun show starts?" I sit up on the bed and cross my legs as if I'm getting ready for a movie marathon.

Archer chuckles. "This is where you strip for me."

"And miss the show? Nah, I think I'm good here."

He moves in, placing his hands on the bed, his mouth barely a breath from mine. "What do I need to do to motivate you?" He kisses the corner of my mouth.

"That helps," I murmur.

"You want me to kiss you?" His lips slowly trail across my cheek. "Is that what you want? My lips pressed to yours?"

His voice is so damn sexy it sends shivers of desire racing down my spine. "Yes. That. I'll take that."

The words are barely out of my mouth before his lips are on mine. It's a soft press, a gentle swipe of his tongue, but it's still sexy and intoxicating. I open for him, wanting more, needing more, but he pulls away.

"I need you naked, Scarlett. There are so many ways I need to kiss you. So many ways to trail your skin with my tongue." He demonstrates this by licking a small path up my neck. "So many places that I need to taste you." He nips at my ear.

"But I'll miss the show."

He stands to his full height and tugs at his shirt. Buttons fly across the room as he pulls the sleeves off his arms and lets the fabric fall to the floor. His heated stare burns into me. "Your turn."

I swallow hard because, damn. This man in a button-down dress shirt is off-the-charts sexy. Seeing this man shirtless is a life-altering experience. Seriously, I've never seen a man more chiseled, more defined. At least not in person. He needs to be in magazines. My hands itch to run to the kitchen to grab my camera.

He cradles my jaw in his large, strong hands. "What's going through that head of yours?"

"I want to take your picture." My voice is thick, but I manage to get the words out.

"Right now?"

I shake my head. "But I want to. Will you let me?"

"I'm pretty sure there's not much I would say no to where you're concerned."

"You just met me."

"Yeah," he agrees but doesn't say more.

"I just—" I lift my hands and place both palms flat on his chest. I don't finish my thought because the feel of his hot, smooth skin beneath my fingertips has me losing all train of thought.

"You just what?"

"I see things differently. My world is through a lens."

"You can take my picture anytime you want. However, they're only for you. No one else."

"Really?" Even I can hear the excitement in my voice.

"Like I said, I can't say no to you."

"What if I said that I wanted to finish undressing you?"

He holds his hands out to his sides and nods. I've never had a man be so open and willing with me. He's truly letting me set the pace, and my mind is going crazy with all the things I want to do to him. With him. I lick my lips at the thought, and my mouth goes dry.

"Those lips." He moves his hand to run the rough pad of his thumb across them.

"Are about to do work." I transfer my hands to the waistband of his dress pants and quickly release the button, lowering the zipper. Without an ounce of hesitation, I reach into his tight black boxer briefs and palm his erection. It's hot and heavy in my hand. My mouth waters. Tugging the boxer briefs, I pull him from the confines of the material and lick the tip. He groans. The reverberation is thick and sounds as if it's torn from the back of his throat.

I smile as I take him into my mouth.

Chapter 3

ARCHER

M Y GROAN REVERBERATES AROUND THE room. Closing my eyes, I tilt my head back. Her mouth is hot. Wet. Her tongue feels like silk against my cock. I force myself to open my eyes. I don't want to miss a minute of Scarlett with her lips wrapped around me.

My hands find their way to her hair, and I fist her strands, holding them tightly in my grip to keep her hair out of her face. The red locks are soft against my calloused hands. It's just as beautiful as she is, but I don't need a single fucking thing blocking my view of this woman.

I should have brought her camera in here with us. She claims that she lives her life through a lens. She should see herself like this. Her green eyes are blazing with desire. Her cheeks are hollow and pink. Her long red locks are wrapped in my hands, not enough to hurt her, but enough for her to know that it's happening. She moans, and my cock twitches in her mouth.

Fuck.

I don't want to come like this. If I only get one night with her, this is not how it's going to go down. It takes everything I have in me to take a step back. She whines in protest as my cock falls from her lips, bouncing against my stomach.

"Stand up." It comes out as a command, and she instantly climbs to her feet as she wipes her mouth with the back of her hand. Gripping my cock, I stroke myself leisurely. I'm aching to be inside her. "Lose the clothes, Firecracker." Taking a step over to the nightstand, I reach inside the top drawer and grab an unopened box of condoms. Like I said, it's been a while. I check the date, just to be sure. I'm turned on beyond belief, but being safe is always a priority. I don't want babies until it's with my wife. Simple as that.

By the time my eyes are back on her, she's standing before me naked. I take my time, letting my gaze roam over her. Her tits are full and round, her hard nipples begging for my touch. Her belly is flat, but her hips flare just enough to bring a man to his knees. Her long tan legs that were wrapped around me earlier are a memory I'll never forget.

"You still with me?" I ask.

"You backing out on me, Kincaid?" she teases.

"No. But if you want to, you say the word." Consent is important to me, and I'm a bossy bastard on my best days, at least in the bedroom. I need to make sure she understands that if she wants to end this, we end it. She has the control here.

"Less talking, more... other stuff," she says with a saucy grin.

"Yes, ma'am." Placing my hands on her hips, I lift her into the air. She smiles down at me, and I have to kiss her. "Latch on, baby." I don't need to say anything else for her to understand. I pull her closer, and her legs wrap around my waist.

I bite down on my cheek when I feel her pussy, hot and wet against my skin. Her arms are around my neck, and I grip her thighs. "I need those lips."

"These lips?" she asks, kissing me just beneath my ear.

"These too," I say, pulling her closer and rubbing her pussy over my abs. I'm right there, my cock hitting her ass. One little jut of my hips, and I'd be inside her. Fuck me, I should have suited up as soon as I confirmed the condoms were still good.

"Didn't your momma ever teach you it's not nice to tease?" she says while her lips trail over my neck to my cheek, to the corner of my mouth.

"I'm a sure thing," I tell her.

She pulls back. Her green eyes are twinkling. "Prove it."

"You can't rush perfection, Firecracker." I move to the bed and lay her down. I'm leaning over her, my hands still on the backs of her thighs, and her arms and legs are still wrapped around me while her back is to the mattress.

"Too many words. Not enough action."

"Must be the red hair," I muse, kissing her lips. It's just a small peck. Nothing compared to what I actually want from her, but I can't let myself get carried away. "It's just us here, Firecracker. Let me hear you."

One night.

I'm taking my time.

I tap her thigh. "Relax for me, beautiful." She does as I say and releases her legs from around my hips and her arms from around my neck. I drop to my knees, and she lifts up on her elbows to watch me.

"You don't have to do that," she says quickly. "We can just skip to the good parts."

I stop and stare at her. "Scarlett, this is the good part. It's all the good part. Whoever you've been with before me that didn't make that known is an asshole. Now lie back and let me taste."

Taking my time, I lift one long leg, trailing my lips from her foot all the way to her inner thigh, before placing it over my shoulder. I repeat the process with the other leg. She squirms but remains silent other than her labored breathing. I shimmy in close, pulling her ass to the edge of the bed.

"So pretty," I whisper. She's shaved, except for a small little strip. My cock aches for release as I move in close, allowing my hot breath to ghost over her clit before letting my tongue take over. The first taste of her explodes on my tongue, and I'm hooked.

I get lost in her, the sounds she's making. The way her legs tighten around my neck. Her hands are pulling my hair, and the way she lifts her hips, seeking out my mouth, guiding me to exactly where she wants me.

All of it.

I take all of it. All of her. Nothing else matters at this moment except for her falling apart on my tongue.

"Archer—" she starts, but she can't even finish her sentence.

Her legs grow tighter around my head. My cock hangs heavy between my thighs. She's close. Fuck, I'm close. I need her to come so that I get my turn. She's first. Always. When I slide one long digit inside her, she makes a sound that's a mix between a mewl and a growl, and my cock twitches, begging to get in on the action.

Almost.

I pump a second digit inside while working her clit with my tongue, and she screams out my name. Her legs quiver around my neck as she grips my hair so tightly, I'm certain I'll lose a few strands.

Worth it.

Once her body falls back to the bed, I slowly remove my fingers and place a kiss on her swollen pussy. I look up to see her lying with her arm over her eyes, and her chest rapidly rising with each breath she pulls into her lungs. Her skin is flushed a light pink, and I know I've never in my life seen anything more beautiful. I take a minute to just stare and memorize her. This moment.

Her arm falls away from her eyes, and she lifts her head. A lazy grin lifts her lips. I need to kiss her. I stand and brace my hands on the bed next to her head and drop my mouth to hers. I trace her lips with my tongue, her taste still clinging to me, but she doesn't seem to mind. She locks her hands behind my neck and pulls me closer.

We're not in a hurry. Sure, my cock is throbbing, but the wait will be worth it. I want to experience every part of her, and right now, it's her tongue sliding against mine as we explore each other's mouths.

It's not until her hand roams over my chest and grips my cock that I pull away from the kiss. "Your hands feel like silk," I mumble before taking a hard nipple into my mouth. Her back arches off the bed.

"You've shown me what a mouth can do," she says, her voice soft and raspy. "Show me what your cock can do."

"Yes, ma'am." Pushing back, I stand and grab the condoms I left on the nightstand. I tear one open and sheath my cock in record time. When I lift my head to tell her to climb up the bed, she's standing next to me.

"On the bed, Popeye."

My cock twitches. "You taking the reins, Firecracker?"

Her eyes glance down at my cock that's hard and angry and more than ready to be inside her. "Yeah," she says, breathless. She clears her throat. "On the bed."

I've never been with a woman who wanted to take charge. It's hot as fuck. I waste no time doing as this vixen demands and crawl to the middle of the bed. I place my hands behind my head and smile at her. "You got me here. Now what are you going to do with me?" I smirk, and she licks her lips.

My heart is pounding in my chest, and my cock is so hard it hurts. I try to remember a time I've ever been this hard. Not just my cock, but me on my own. I don't know that I've been this desperate, this ready to be inside a woman.

Scarlett climbs onto the bed one knee at a time. Her tits sway as she moves, and my mouth waters for another taste. "Remember what I said, Kincaid," she taunts as she tosses one leg over my hips and settles back on my thighs. I reach for her, gripping her tight. I just need to be tethered to her in some way.

"What's that?" I ask. I'm not thinking clearly when all I can think about is her pussy strangling my cock.

"Don't fall in love with me."

"What about your pussy?" I ask, smirking. I keep one hand on her hip while the other traces through her folds. "Can I fall in love with your pussy?" Not that I would. I know what this is, what tonight is about, and I'm okay with that. However, the question spewed from my lips before I could stop it.

She laughs. Not just a "ha-ha, you're funny" laugh. No, this one is a full-body laugh. The kind that shakes your entire body, head tilted back as you let it all out.

Loud.

Uninhibited.

Fucking beautiful.

"Why don't you sample the goods before you decide that?" she teases.

"Oh, baby, we're going to do better than sample." I press my thumb to her clit, and she moans, rocking her hips forward for more friction. "We're going to test drive."

"That's fine," she says, grabbing my cock with her hands. "But I'm driving."

She lifts up on her knees, inches forward, and guides my cock inside her. I grip her hips tightly, so tight, in fact, I could possibly leave bruises on her creamy white skin, but she doesn't seem to mind, and I can't seem to let go.

I don't *want* to let go.

Scarlett is in complete control. I don't know her well enough yet to determine if she needs to be the one guiding us or if she just decided she wanted to work me over. Whatever the reason, although I'm leaning toward the latter, I'm here for it.

Once I'm buried all the way inside her, she stops and smiles down at me. Her long red hair hangs over one shoulder, and my heart actually skips a fucking beat at the sight of her. "What are you thinking about right now? You've got this look on your face. I can't describe it."

"My cock is inside you, and you want to chat?" I raise an eyebrow.

The vixen wiggles her hips, and I moan, my grip on her waist growing even tighter. "Just tell me what you're thinking."

"I'm thinking that you look like a fucking goddess impaled on my cock. You feel even better."

"Sweet nothings," she muses with a grin.

"Don't fall in love with me." I shoot her words back at her, and her smile grows.

"I don't fall in love, Kincaid."

"Neither do I. Now, I thought you were driving. Do you need some help?"

She leans forward, her palms resting on my pecs. Her nails dig into my skin, sure to leave a mark, but I couldn't care less. "I can navigate just fine." She doesn't need to say more because she lifts her hips and slams them back down. I bite down on my cheek as I take everything that she's willing to give me.

It doesn't take long for her to set a rhythm. She closes her eyes and tilts her head back, allowing herself to get lost in the moment while I get lost in her. I'm not even sure I blink, because I don't want to miss any part of my time with her.

She's intoxicating.

"Archer." She moans my name. No, it's more than just a moan. It's as if she's speaking another language, one that only she and I understand, as she continues to make sounds and mumble under her breath.

"So good," she pants.

I raise my hips and help lift her from my cock, bringing her back down, and her pussy squeezes me like a vise. "Fuck, that feels good."

"I'm close."

Thank fuck. "Are you going to come on my cock?"

"Mmhmm."

"Tell me, Scarlett. I want to hear you say it. Tell me you're going to come all over my cock." I lift my hips as she's coming down with hers, causing her hands to dig even deeper into my skin.

"I—I'm going to c—come on your—" She doesn't get to finish as she shatters around me. I feel her body pulsing from the inside, and it's the sexiest fucking thing ever. There has been nothing sweeter than watching this headstrong woman fall apart while I'm inside her.

She leans forward, resting on my chest, while I'm still buried balls deep. My cock throbs for release, but I'm going to give her a minute to get her breathing under control. Her hot breath puffs out against my chest as I slowly rake my hands up and down her bare back.

"You good?" I ask.

"Best. Sex. Ever," she says, not bothering to lift her head.

"We're not done yet."

"I need a breather."

"That's fine. I'll do all the work."

"Wait?" She lifts her head. "Did you come?"

"No. I was waiting for you."

"You should have come with me."

"Then I wouldn't get to do this." I flip us over so that she's now on her back, and I'm nestled between her thighs. "Grab the sheets or grab me. Hell, grab the bed. I don't care what you hold on to, but you're going to want to hold on."

She opens her mouth, I'm sure to question me, but the look in my eyes must stop her. She nods, slides her hands under my arms and grips my back.

"Good girl." I slowly pull out and slam back in. Over and over at a punishing pace, I fuck her. It's hard and fast, and the bite of her nails into my skin encourages me to go faster. To thrust harder.

"Oh, shit!" she cries out, and I feel another orgasm tear through her.

That's all it takes, and I shoot off into the condom. For a fleeting second, I wish the barrier wasn't between us. I've never even considered that before, but something tells me that sex without a barrier with the lovely Scarlett would be life-altering.

Who am I kidding? Sex with a barrier was life-altering.

Carefully, I pull out of her and remove the condom, tossing it in the trash can next to the bed. Dropping down beside her, I pull her into my arms before reaching behind me for the cover to drag it over us.

"I should go," she says sleepily.

"You should stay. Nap, and we can do this again when you wake up."

"I'm leaving, Archer."

"I know, Firecracker."

"You wanna be my hookup buddy?" There's humor in her tired voice.

"You have a lot of those, do you?"

"No, but after that performance, I think we should consider it. As long as you can refrain from falling in love with me."

"I'm already in love with your pussy." To prove my point, I run my fingers through her sensitive folds.

"I think the feeling is mutual," she moans.

As much as I hate to, I pull my hand away. She needs rest. We both do. "Sleep."

"Okay, buddy." She pats my chest, and her body relaxes into me.

Closing my eyes with a beautiful woman in my arms and a sated smile on my face is not how I saw the night ending, but I'm damn sure not going to complain about this turn of events.

Chapter
4

SCARLETT

I JOLT AWAKE. MY BODY is covered in sweat, and my breathing is labored. There is also a noticeable wetness between my thighs, accompanied by an ache that just won't go away. The same ache that's been lingering for weeks. Swiping my sweaty hair out of my eyes, I focus on taking deep, even breaths.

It was just a dream.

It will be five weeks tomorrow since I laid eyes on Archer Kincaid, yet he still haunts me in my sleep. Okay, not so much haunts them as much as he lives there. Rent-free, I might add. It's not enough that I think about my night with him every single day. I have to relive the moment in my dreams too.

That night was hands down the best sex of my life. We fell asleep, only for Archer to wake me up a few hours later to ravish me. Seriously, his hands and his mouth seemed to be everywhere all at once, and all I could do was let him take me along for the ride. Besides, it was only fair that he got a turn driving the sex train since I already had mine.

I'm not a stranger to hookups. No, I've had my fair share. I don't do the "let's get close and get to know each other" thing. I've lost too many people I love in my life to lose any more. The pain isn't worth the connection.

However, my night with Archer is one I can't seem to shake, no matter how hard I try. The memory haunts me. It's never been an issue for me before. I could take the emotions out of the act. I think he broke me. Archer Kincaid broke me, and I don't know what to do about it.

Turning my head to the side, I peer at the alarm clock. It's just after six. I don't have to be at the studio until nine, but there is no way I'm getting back to sleep after that dream. Trust me, I've tried after each and every dream, and it never works. So not only am I sexually frustrated, but I'm also losing precious sleep.

Something has got to give.

Tossing off the covers, I gingerly climb out of bed and stretch my arms up high. I need to get out. I need to meet new people and stop staying held up in my apartment every night. The dreams have to stop. The constant replay of that night has to stop. I make a mental note to talk to Palmer today about places to go outside of Willow River. The last thing I need is to run into *him*. To be honest, that's why I've been staying in, but that's not me. None of this is me.

It's time to take back my life.

I will not let a one-night stand control me.

Hottest sex of my life be damned.

"Thank you so much, Scarlett."

"You're most welcome. It was a pleasure to get to photograph this handsome little guy." Sara, my client, just beams down at her newborn son.

"We'll call to schedule his appointment next month. I want a session once a month for a year to show his growth. I saw it online and loved the idea. Thankfully, Palmer is giving me a discount." She laughs.

"Well, we will be here when you're ready for us." I walk to the door and hold it open for her as we wave goodbye.

The door closes, and I take a deep breath. The studio is silent for the first time all day. I've got to admit, I wasn't sure how I'd feel about studio photography when my heart has been with outdoor landscapes, but I really enjoy it. I love getting to work with the families and document special occasions and milestones in their lives. I was sure I'd be bored by now, but that's not the case.

The chime above the door rings out, and I turn to see who it is. There's a break in the schedule, so I'm not expecting anyone. I smile when I see Palmer with Remi on her hip. "Hey, you two. What are you doing here?" I ask my boss. She's more than that. Palmer has become a friend in a very short amount of time. She's so down-to-earth and easy to work for. Another aspect that makes me enjoy my job.

"We just had lunch with Daddy," Palmer says, bouncing Remi on her hip.

"Remi, did you see Daddy?" I ask the adorable little girl. She just smiles as she chews on a small toy that looks like a banana with handles.

"Brooks has been working a ton of hours. He's helping to cover for a coworker who just became a grandma for the first time. He's worked the last three weekends because he took her shifts on."

"That was sweet of him."

"Yeah." A soft smile pulls at Palmer's lips. "He's just a big old teddy bear. Right, baby?" She beams at her daughter, who is jabbering away as if she's part of the conversation.

"Anyway," Palmer says, looking up at me. "I know you've got things handled here. I'm not checking up on you." She gives me a kind smile.

"Nothing wrong with it if you were." I return her grin.

She waves her hand that's not holding Remi in the air. "You know what you're doing. I stopped to invite you over to our place this weekend. Brooks has been working so much I'm having everyone over for dinner."

"Oh, I don't want to impose on family time." Although, I'd love to see Archer again. I wonder if he's up for a repeat of our night together. We said a benefits arrangement, but I haven't heard from him. Then again, I haven't reached out either. A wave of desire hits me, and I shift my stance to alleviate that ache between my thighs.

I've never had this reaction to just thinking about a man. I'm definitely going to need to convince him to go another round.

"Girl, the more, the merrier. It's nothing fancy. I'm just going to order pizza. I was going to grill, but it's supposed to rain and be cold tomorrow."

It's on the tip of my tongue to refuse again, but I really do want to see Archer. Even if I can't convince him to spend another night with me, the eye candy from him and his brothers will make my night. I was supposed to be asking Palmer about places to go outside of Willow River for a night out, but no way am I passing up the chance to see Archer and the entire Kincaid gang. The ladies are cool and, well, eye candy.

"What can I bring?" I ask with more enthusiasm than necessary.

Palmer grins. "Nothing. Just you. Oh, I mean, unless there is a drink you'd like. We always have someone who stays sober to give rides home, or you're welcome to stay at ours. I know my sisters-in-law are planning to have a drink or five." Palmer giggles, which in turn makes Remi giggle as she mimics her momma. "It's been too damn long since a lot of us were able to drink. Crosby is the only one who's sitting out this round. For the rest of us mommas, it's a pump and dump weekend." She winks.

"Well, I'll think of something. What time?"

"Be at ours around six, or you're more than welcome to come earlier and just hang out."

"Thank you, Palmer. I was planning to ask you the best places to go outside of Willow River."

"We go to Harris a lot. It's about twenty minutes from here. They have a mall and a ton more to do there. We should plan a girls' day. We can show you around."

"Really? That would be great." I'm used to spending most of my time alone, but the idea of hanging out with Palmer and her friends and family for a girls' day is more appealing than I ever thought it would be. There is just something about this little town and the people in it. It's charming and welcoming.

"Great. We can talk to everyone tomorrow night and make plans."

"Thank you." I smile at her.

"All right, well, we're going to head out. We have to grab some groceries and then go home and take a nap."

"Oh, before you go, the prints for the Jacobson family came in earlier. Do you want to see them?"

"Yes. Oh my goodness. That was such a fun shoot. Three boys under three, that momma has her hands full, but they were sweet as pie," she says as she follows me to the back room of the studio to look at the prints.

Since Palmer is holding Remi, I carefully remove the prints from their packaging and lay them out on the table. "These are amazing."

"Those littles were so fun to shoot. I know some are hesitant to do family photography, but kids just want to have fun. The candid shots are the best, and memories these families will always cherish."

"I was one of those people," I confess. "But family photography definitely keeps you on your toes, and with such a small town, we get weddings, and birthdays, and engagements, and it's more than I anticipated, but I'm glad you gave me a chance."

"Who knows, maybe your one-year contract will turn into more." She gives me a kind, hopeful smile, and I return it.

"I enjoy it, but my heart is with the landscape," I tell her.

"We have some beautiful landscapes here in Georgia."

"Are you trying to persuade me?" I laugh.

"Yep. I've got less than a year to make you fall in love with this town and all we have to offer."

"The town is amazing. You've been so good to me, but traveling is where my passion lies."

"I hear ya." Palmer grins. "I'm a small-town girl, and you're not. There's nothing wrong with that. However, that doesn't mean I'm not going to keep trying to get you to stay in our sleepy little town."

"It's hard to settle down when you don't have family holding you in place," I tell her.

Palmer's eyes soften. I told her a little about my backstory during my interview. "You mentioned your parents had passed."

"Yeah. I was adopted," I tell her. "Only child and my parents were both only children and not close to any of their extended family. It's just me." I shrug.

"Scarlett."

I can hear what she doesn't say just from the tone of her voice. She's sorry, she feels bad for me, and the sadness in her eyes says it all.

"That's life, right?" I say with another shrug. I have to act as though I'm over it, or I'll get lost in the grief. "That's when I decided life was too short not to live each day how you want to. Traveling, it's best for me. I love it. I love seeing new places and meeting new people. I love capturing the world with my camera."

"We have a lot of family we can share with you." She smiles softly.

It's on the tip of my tongue to tell her that her brother-in-law has already been very welcoming and giving, but I bite my tongue. Palmer and I have grown close, but I'm certain she wouldn't appreciate me telling her about my sexcapades with Archer.

"Thanks, kind of you. I'm good, I promise. We're not all blessed with large families, and that's okay."

"You've only been in town a few weeks, and as far as I know, the only interaction you've had with my family is at the wedding, of which you were working, and if someone has stopped by the studio. We're loud, we're opinionated, and we love hard." She chuckles. "The Kincaids, my husband's family, they have a motto. Work hard and love harder. They live by that. And there is a lot of love to go around."

"Well, I'm looking forward to all of that while I'm here."

She points at me. "I'm going to wear you down, Scarlett Hatfield."

This time it's me who's chuckling. "I appreciate the sentiment, but I wasn't meant to be in one place for too long." I don't add that even my birth parents didn't want me, I keep that locked up tight. I don't know much about them. Just that they both signed away their rights. I never wanted to know. Jack and Tiffany Hatfield were my parents. They were the family that wanted me, and that was enough for me.

"Tomorrow. Six. I'll text you my address."

"Thank you, Palmer. I'm looking forward to a night of getting to know your family."

"Is this where I should apologize?" She looks down at Remi and kisses the top of her head. "I have four single brothers-in-law. Archer and Ryder are pretty tame. Ryder is taken, kind of. It's a long story. Archer is single, and so are the twins, Maverick and Merrick, the babies of the family. The twins will flirt with you and be over the top about it. So, yeah, I apologize in advance."

"I can handle it," I assure her. I don't know how I manage to contain my smile at hearing that Archer is still single. In the back of my mind, I knew it was a possibility he'd met someone, which is why I hadn't heard from him.

"Oh, I have no doubt. I just wanted you to be aware of what you're getting yourself into."

"I appreciate that." I hold my hand out for Remi, and she grabs hold of my finger. "I'll see you later, sweet girl." I smile at her. She rests her head on her mommy's shoulder but offers me a grin, showing off her two front teeth.

"I'll get out of your hair. Do you have any more sessions scheduled for today?"

"Nothing on the books. I'm hoping to use the time to get some edits done."

"Hopefully it will be a quiet last couple of hours for you."

"If not, I can do it this weekend. It's not like I have a banging social life."

"Hey, this weekend you do." She gives me a stern look, one I'm sure Remi will see many times in her lifetime. "You better not bail on me."

"Yes, boss," I tease.

"You're going to fit in just fine," she assures me. With a smile and a wave, she and Remi head back out the way they came in.

After filling up my water bottle, I settle in to work on some edits from today's sessions. I think back to my tenth birthday when my parents bought me my first camera. I fell in love with capturing all the moments in our life. It became my passion. I'm lucky to be able to do what I love. I know my mom used to say, do what you love, and it will never feel like work. I guess I took that to heart. I'd like to think I'm honoring her memory and her advice by pursuing my dream and my love of photography.

That dream led me to Willow River. I went back and forth with my decision to sign a one-year employment contract, but I'm so glad I did. I have a feeling I'm never going to forget my time spent here in Willow River. Without a doubt, I'll never forget the residents.

I smile when I think about Archer. As long as I live, I'll never forget our night together. Best sex of my life, hands down, but it was more than just the sex. He was good to me and let me take control without question. Archer Kincaid is a sexy, gentle giant, and I can only hope that I get to spend more time with him while I'm here.

Willow River
Georgia

WILLOW RIVER, GA · HOME OF THE KINCAID BROTHERS · WILLOW RIVER, GA · HOME OF THE KINCAID BROTHERS ·

WWW.KAYLEERYAN.COM

Chapter
5

ARCHER

"**G**IMME." I HOLD MY ARMS out for my niece to steal her away from my brother. "Come to Uncle Archer," I tell Remi. She giggles and reaches for me.

"I've been working a ton of hours and just want time with my daughter," Brooks grumbles.

"Well, guess what? I'm two hours early. That means Remi and I are going to play and turn up one of those princess movies she loves way too loud, and you can go spend some time with your wife."

His face lights up with a smile. "You were always my favorite brother," he says, already moving down the hall to find his wife, Palmer.

"I'm going to tell the others that you said that!" I call after him. I bounce Remi in my arms. "Your daddy is silly." I tickle her sides, and her baby girl giggles fill my heart.

Being one of nine Kincaid brothers means there is never a dull moment in our lives. Over the last few years, my brothers have been getting married and adding babies, expanding our family. I'm not the middle brother, but I'm not the youngest either. Ryder and the twins Maverick and Merrick are younger than me, and then we have Orrin, Declan, Brooks, Sterling, and Rushton, who are older than me. We're all pretty much stair-stepped in age, and I try not to think about what that meant for my parents.

No kid should ever have to think about *that*.

"What are we going to watch?" I ask my niece. She just smiles as she places her hands on my cheeks and gives me a sloppy kiss. "I love you too." I laugh, wiping my lips.

"It's warm out today. How about we go for a walk?" I move to the front hallway and open the closet door where I know Brooks and Palmer keep the stroller. I put Remi's jacket on her. It's warm out, but still, the wind adds a little chill to the air. I wheel her back to the living room to grab the diaper bag I remember was sitting next to the couch. I do a quick check. Toys, blanket, diapers, wipes, and a bottle. It should be good for a short little stroll around the neighborhood.

Pulling my phone out of my jeans pocket, I shoot Brooks a text. Being the nice brother that I am, I keep it out of the group thread we have with our brothers.

Me: Taking Remi for a stroll around the block.

I follow it with a winking emoji. I laugh when I read his reply.

Brooks: You're my favorite.

"Your daddy just told me I was his favorite. That's twice in one day. Make sure you tell the others, okay, Rem?" I tap her on the nose with my index finger. "You ready to stroll?"

Remi claps her hands. This kid, she's always so happy. I knew coming over early was a good idea. Not only because I knew Brooks and Palmer wanted time together but because I was driving myself crazy sitting in my house thinking about Scarlett. It's been five weeks since I've laid eyes on her. Since I've felt and tasted her skin. Five weeks of looking for her every time I drove through town and trying to think of a way to ask Palmer for her number without tipping everyone in my family off that we slept together. When Palmer called last night to tell me about today, she casually mentioned that Scarlett would be coming as well.

I've barely slept.

I feel like teenage Archer, excited to go to school to see the girl I was crushing on. Finally, I decided that some one-on-one time with my niece was exactly what I needed. I work long hours this time of year, too, and I don't get to spend as much time with my family as I'd like. However, I always try my best to make it when something like this comes up. My brothers, all eight of them, are my best friends. Their wives too. And their kids, well, let's just say being an uncle kicks ass.

Maneuvering the stroller out onto the front porch, I lock the front door behind me. It's a keyless entry, and I have the code. Hell, we all have the codes or copies of keys to each other's houses. That's just what we do.

"All right, Rem, let's do this." I carry the stroller down the steps, and once it's back on the sidewalk, we head off down the street. Remi laughs and points using her baby jabbers, and it makes me smile.

My mind drifts to Scarlett, but I'm too busy replying to Remi, even though I have no idea what she's saying to get lost in my thoughts. This is exactly what I needed. My guess is that Brooks would be in agreement about now.

Remi is having such a great time, and it's a nice day, I decide to go another block before turning around. I take my time, taking smaller steps and stopping to let Remi grab a flower from a nearby flowerpot. Thankfully, she doesn't shove it into her mouth, and I don't have to take it from her. She's the only baby I know that doesn't shove every item they pick up into their mouths. Blakely, Declan's daughter, was terrible about it as a baby. Anytime I watched her for him, I felt like I needed to hold her to keep her from grabbing something random and putting it in her mouth.

By the time we make it back to the house, an hour has passed, and Remi is passed out in her stroller. I carry it up the steps and quietly type in the code. The house is quiet when I walk inside, so I carefully take Remi from her stroller and make my way to the couch. I know that I could put her down in her room or even in the Pack 'N Play in the corner, but I'd rather snuggle with her. Once my brothers get here, I'll have to share. That's okay, though. I'll be able to steal hugs from Blakely, Declan's oldest, who is almost six, which is hard to believe. His son, Beckham, is just a few months old, and then there's Orion. He's Orrin's son, and he's just a couple of months old. I'm not sure if Palmer and Deacon's sister Piper will be here, but if she is, her little girl, Penelope, is close in age to Orion and Beckham. There will be lots of babies, but there are a lot of us too.

I'm going to enjoy my snuggle time before it gets interrupted. Settling back on the couch, I keep one hand on Remi's back as I close my eyes and listen to her soft breaths. I don't know how long we're lying here when I hear footsteps on the hardwood floor. I crack open one eye to see Brooks taking a seat next to me on the couch.

"Want me to take her?" he asks.

"Nah, she's fine."

"If you're sure, I'm going to go help Palmer set up."

"I thought we were just ordering pizza."

He grins. "You know my wife. Hell, all of our sisters-in-law are just like Mom. They'd rather have too much than not enough. She made brownies and some kind of strawberry dessert that will make your mouth water just by looking at it."

"Just keep it down, will you? Me and my girl are trying to nap." I close my eyes and listen as his soft chuckle follows him into the kitchen.

Remi stirs in my arms, which jolts me awake. I glance down at her, and she's just starting to wake up as she rubs her eyes. I place a kiss on the top of her head, and a feminine "Aw" has me turning to look for the source of the voice. To my surprise, Scarlett is sitting in the chair, watching us, with a soft expression on her face.

"Hey," I croak, my voice heavy with sleep. "I didn't mean to fall asleep."

"Looks like you two needed it." She nods toward Remi.

"We took a walk, and it must have worn us both out." I sit up, which has Remi lifting her head. She smiles, and my heart constricts in my chest. Damn, I love this kid. "Hey, baby girl," I say softly. "You feel better after your nap?"

Remi babbles back, and I grin.

"You're good with her."

"She's a good baby."

Scarlett nods. "That might be, but babies are a good judge of character. She knows that she can trust you."

"Of course she can. I'd never let anything happen to her." Now that I'm more alert, I can see that my memory of the lovely Scarlett didn't do her justice.

Scarlett smiles softly. "She's lucky to have you."

The front door opens, and I know immediately that it's Declan and his family when I hear tiny feet racing on the hardwood floor.

"Blake!" Declan calls after his daughter. "Take your shoes off and stop running in the house."

"Uncle Brooks and Aunt Palmer let me," Blakely calls back, making me laugh.

I feel a hand slap at the back of my head. "Just wait until you have a sassy almost six-year-old who thinks she's going on sixteen. I'll remind you of this moment."

"I'd like to think I've learned from all of our mistakes." I turn my attention back to Scarlett. "Blakely was the only grandchild, the only niece up until this little beauty was born. We kind of went out of our way to spoil her rotten."

"You've learned nothing," Declan says as he leans down and takes Remi from my arms.

"Hey, baby hog."

"Here, have another." Kennedy, Declan's wife, walks into the room and hands me their son, Beckham.

"There's my little man." I take him from his momma and snuggle him close. Beckham wiggles until he's comfortable resting against my shoulder.

"Are you some kind of baby whisperer or something?" Scarlett asks.

"They all are," Palmer says as she comes into the room. "All of them, even their dad, Raymond. It's like it's in their genes or something." She laughs.

"There are lots of things we excel at," I say, my eyes meeting Scarlett's. She blushes, and I have to bite down on my cheek to hide my smile. Maybe I can pull her to the side and convince her to come home with me tonight.

"What he said," Brooks says, pulling Palmer onto his lap.

"What time is it?" I ask, kissing the top of Beckham's head. There's nothing quite like the smell of a baby. Well, when they're not shitting or puking, that is.

"Just after six."

I'm getting ready to ask if everyone else is still on their way when the door opens, and the chaos begins. Within ten minutes, all eight of my brothers, their wives, and kids are here. It's loud and boisterous, and I love it. I couldn't imagine not having our big, crazy family.

"Are Mom and Dad coming?" Sterling asks. He's standing behind his wife, Alyssa, with her back pressed to his front.

"No. Dad's taking her to Harris to dinner and a movie."

"Are you still going to take me to dinner and a movie after we've been married as long as they have?" This comes from Crosby, Rushton's wife.

"Yes," me and my brothers reply for him. The entire room erupts with laughter.

"Scarlett," Palmer says, "something you should know about the Kincaid men. They love hard."

"Once they fall, it's like a skyscraper crashing to the ground," Alyssa says. Sterling pinches her side, which has her laughing and wiggling, trying to escape his hold, but we all know that's not going to happen. He'll always hold on to her. It took them some time to get to their happily ever after, and Sterling won't ever let another day pass where Alyssa doesn't know what she means to him. Doesn't matter they're newly married. Hell, Orrin, Brooks, Declan, Rushton, Sterling, and Dad, all married Kincaid men who are willing to shout their love for their wives from the rooftops.

They want the world to know.

Not that I blame them. If I had that kind of love, I'd be on board for my own shouting confessions on rooftops.

"We're talking huge explosion," Maverick chimes in. "Lots of smoke, super tall building," he says, placing his hand over Orrin's head where he's standing next to Jade, who is holding their son, Orion.

"Crumbled like a cookie, the lot of them," Merrick jokes.

"Just wait," Rushton tells them. "You're going to be the one crumbling after the love of a good woman. Don't worry. As your older brothers, we'll be sure to remind you of this conversation."

Maverick and Merrick, the twins and the babies of the family, just laugh it off. The doorbell rings, and they both move to answer it. Without jostling Beckham, I manage to reach into my wallet and grab a twenty and hand it to Declan. He's already got one from his own wallet in his hands. We all like to pitch in on nights like this. There are a lot of us, and I know the bill for the pizza is going to be huge.

Sure enough, Maverick and Merrick come walking in with four pizzas each in their hands, with Palmer following along behind them.

"They're kind of handy to have around," she teases. The twins set the pizzas on the kitchen counter and come back to where we're all gathered in the living room.

"You know we're better looking than Brooks," Maverick jokes. "We're happy to be the eye candy to you that our brother can't be."

"You might be the same size as us now, but there are more of us."

"Five married, and four single. I think we can take you," Merrick quips.

"Hey now." I shake my head at him. "This is your fight."

"Come on, man. Us single guys have to stick together. Ryder?" Maverick asks.

"You're on your own, Mav," Ryder tells him. "We all know I've already crumbled."

Maverick nods. "What's your excuse?"

"Do I need one?"

"Single brothers unite." Merrick thrusts his fist into the air. We all laugh at their antics.

"I'm single, but that's just because I haven't met anyone who can make me crumble." There's a brief moment where the lovely Scarlett pops in my head, but she's leaving. Her time here in Willow River is temporary, and this is my home.

"I'm disappointed, Archer." Maverick shakes his head as if my words are the craziest thing he's ever heard.

"I'm just saying."

"Give me my nephew." Maverick steps toward me and takes Beckham from my arms. "Don't listen to anything he says, little man. Us single Kincaid men need to stick together."

"Don't be corrupting my son," Kennedy, Declan's wife, warns him.

"Just teaching him the Kincaid way."

"There is only one way, little brother," Orrin speaks up.

Maverick looks down at Beckham. "We work hard, and we love harder, but—" Maverick looks up at Orrin and grins. "Until we find her, we flirt and play, and—" He's cut off when Jade, Orrin's wife, smacks the back of his head. "Ouch."

"Don't be teaching him that."

"Tell your momma I'm right, Orion," Maverick tells our other nephew, who's just taking us all in. He's a baby, just a few months old, like Beckham.

"Let's eat," Ryder says. He stands from his chair and moves toward the kitchen, with the rest of our family following suit.

As for me, I'm slow to move as I watch Scarlett out of the corner of my eye. When she stands, so do I.

"Are you going to eat?" she asks.

You. She'd probably kick my ass if I said that out loud. "Yeah, let's eat." I place my hand on the small of her back to lead her toward the kitchen. It's an open-floor plan, but I still guide her. It's my excuse to touch her. If the goose bumps that break out across her skin are any kind of indication, she's thinking about our night together.

I bend down. "What are you doing later?"

She stops walking to look over at me. "Going home."

"Wrong answer."

"Going home with you." She smirks, and I have the urge to smack her ass, but I keep my hand where it is on the small of her back.

"Good girl." I want to kiss her. I can still taste her even after all these weeks.

"Just sex," she reminds me.

"Just sex," I confirm. I take a step forward, my hand still on the small of her back, and she moves with me.

We make our plates as if we didn't just make plans to hook up once we leave my family. Glad to know we're both on the same page. Once she's filled her plate, I grab us both a beer at her request and nod toward the living room. We settle in our same seats, and I hate it. I want to sit next to her. However, I know that's just asking for family interference. We don't need them in our business.

I was already excited to get to spend time with my family, but now, knowing that Scarlett is coming home with me, this night just got a whole lot better.

Chapter 6

SCARLETT

"SO, LET ME GET THIS straight. You combine the cash and the pieces of two games so everyone can play?" I ask Alyssa.

She chuckles. "Yeah, they've been doing it for years. A regular game of Monopoly, it's only eight players. There are nine of them."

"Do you ever play with them?" I ask her.

"I did once when we were younger. I spent the entire time laughing. It was more fun to watch them."

"They are definitely entertaining," Crosby says. "None of us ever play, even though they offer. It entertains them for a while, and we get to have girl time." She rubs her small baby bump while looking at her husband and brothers-in-law.

"Archer tried to convince them to combine money from three games. It gets tight with the bank when all nine of them play even with the added money from the second game."

"And you just use one round of the properties?"

"Yep. The only thing we don't use from the second game is the properties and the board. Although, we keep them. Sometimes things get heated, and we've had torn property cards in the past." Palmer chuckles.

"Pay up, fucker!" Merrick holds his hand out to Orrin, who grumbles as he places two one-hundred-dollar bills in the palm of Merrick's hand.

"Damn, I missed it," a deep male voice says.

I turn to look at the newcomer, and I recognize the couple from the wedding.

"Sorry we're late," the woman says. She sees me and smiles. "Scarlett, right? I'm Ramsey, cousin to this brood. This is my husband, Deacon, who is also Palmer's older brother."

"I might need someone to write me a family tree." I laugh.

"We should totally do that," Jade agrees.

"Not a bad idea," Palmer agrees. "Are you all hungry? There's pizza, chips, some dips, and a couple of dessert options."

Ramsey's face scrunches up at the mention of food.

"What's that?" Palmer asks her.

"What's what?" Ramsey asks. Her eyes flash to her husband.

"That look. What was that look?" Palmer asks her. "Best friend, remember. You can't hide from me. What's going on?"

"Told you." Deacon laughs, pulling his wife into his arms and kissing the top of her head.

Palmer claps her hands. "Listen up, people," she says over the sounds of all the guys playing the game. Suddenly the room grows quiet, and all eyes turn toward Palmer, who nods toward Ramsey and Deacon.

They're both smiling. Ramsey turns to look at her husband over her shoulder, and he pecks her lips with a kiss. "Love you," Deacon murmurs. I watch as Ramsey visibly relaxes into his embrace. She turns back to her family, and a slow grin spreads across her face.

"We're pregnant!" she blurts. "Twelve weeks today!"

The only way to describe what happens next is chaos. Chairs are slid back, and everyone is on their feet. Hugs, kisses, handshakes, slaps on the back, and even a few tears are shed as Ramsey and Deacon are embraced by their family, congratulating them on their pregnancy.

"Congratulations," I tell them once the room has calmed down.

"Thank you. We're excited."

"Tink, we're falling behind," Sterling tells his wife.

Alyssa laughs. "Maybe we should do something about that, Tank."

Sterling stands from the table. "Deacon, you can take my spot." He doesn't take his eyes off his wife. Once he reaches her, he bends, lifting her into his arms, bridal style. "We're out," he calls to the room.

Everyone erupts with laughter and a few catcalls. I think they're joking, but Sterling doesn't stop and put her down. He pauses next to the door and leans over for her to grab her purse, and they walk out the door.

"Are they leaving?" I ask Crosby.

She grins. "Yeah. They're leaving."

"Can you blame him?" Rushton asks. "Your wife tells you she's ready for a baby. There isn't time to waste."

"Is that what you did?" I ask him.

"Nah, we created this little one without even trying. That's love," he says, winking at his wife.

"Are we playing?" Merrick asks.

"It's your turn, Mer." Ryder laughs.

"Right." Merrick grins. "Let's do this."

The guys resume the game as the ladies talk about babies, pregnancy, and all the things that I don't know much about. I've never had a lot of close friends. Living in foster care until I was four, I guess I just learned to be a loner. My mom used to tell me that I was shy when they brought me home. It took me some time to warm up to them, and then once I did, I latched on. She always said it was because they became my security. My safe place. They wanted me, and to me, that was enough.

I soak in the feeling of family that surrounds me. I hope everyone in this room knows how incredibly lucky they are to have this kind of connection. They're all close and up in each other's business. I always thought that I would hate that, but I've still longed for it. Seeing it in live action, the way they care and love one another, it's got me all up in my feelings. I'll never have what they have, but it's nice to be able to see the bond between this large, loud family while I'm here.

"Thank you so much for having me," I tell Palmer and Brooks. Everyone is starting to pack up and leave, and it's time that I do the same. I don't know if I'm still going home with Archer. I've been trying to avoid looking at him most of the night. I'm sure they can all see right through me, but no one has said anything.

"You need a ride?" Brooks asks.

"No. I only had one beer, and that was when I first got here." I had one drink with my dinner but stopped soon after. I wanted to make sure that I had my wits about me for later, or now, I guess. If it's still happening. I chance a look at Archer across the room and find his heated stare already on me. I give a slight nod, and his lips tilt into a smile.

Why is that so sexy?

He bobs his head, satisfied with my answer.

"I'm so glad that you came," Palmer says, pulling me into a hug.

"Thank you for including me. It was nice not to sit at home on my own for once."

"Oh, girls' night is on," she tells me. "We forgot to talk about it, but I'll start a group chat with the ladies and include you in it."

I laugh. "That sounds like a plan. I'll see you all later." I wave, then wave at Archer, Ryder, Maverick, and Merrick. The twins are staying here, I overheard, and I think Ryder is too. Everyone else has already left to get their kids home and in bed.

"I'm going too." I hear Archer say.

"You good to drive, man?" Brooks asks him.

"Yeah, I only had half a beer."

"You got a hot date or something?" Brooks teases.

"Nah, just a long week. I have a shit ton to get done around the house tomorrow that I didn't get to today. I worked this morning."

"Damn, bro, I'm sure you're tanked. Be safe driving home. You sure you don't want to stay?" Brooks offers.

"I'm good. I'll text you when I get home."

I don't hear what Brooks says next. I've stalled long enough eavesdropping, so I open the front door and step out onto the front porch. It's a nice night, a little chilly, but summer is right around the corner. I'm excited for all the flowers to start to bloom. My finger practically itches to pull out my camera and document the landscape of this charming, small town.

My foot has barely reached the second step when I hear the front door open and close behind me. I stop and look over my shoulder to find a grinning Archer taking long strides. He reaches the second step and slides his arm around my waist.

"You want to leave your car here or follow me?" he asks once we reach my Subaru.

"I can't leave my car here. They're going to know I went home with you."

"Is that supposed to be a secret?"

"I mean, yeah, don't you think? It's not like we're dating or anything." His expression is neutral, and I wish more than anything I could tell what he's thinking.

"You good to drive?"

"I'm fine. Promise."

"All right. I don't live far. Just about a ten-minute drive. I'll drive slow."

"I can keep up, Kincaid. Just because I'm new in town doesn't mean I don't remember how to get there."

"I think you've already proven that." He winks. Leaning around me, he pulls open the driver's side door and waits for me to climb behind the wheel. He braces his hands on the hood of my car and leans down so he can see me. "Put my number in your phone in case you need me."

"You act like I'm going to war." I laugh.

"Just humor me, Firecracker."

I pretend to be annoyed, but in all honesty, I'm anything but. And that nickname... From anyone else, I would hate it, but when it's from Archer's lips, it almost feels like a warm embrace. "Fine." I reach into my purse for my phone and open a new contact. I nod, letting him know that I'm ready, and he rattles off his phone number.

"Send me a text."

"So bossy," I tease but do as he asks. "You could have just asked me for my number like a normal person." I stick my tongue out at him.

"Hold that thought, beautiful. We'll put that tongue to good use."

"Hmm, I was hoping we could use yours," I reply boldly.

He laughs. It's a deep, throaty sound that intensifies the already throbbing ache between my thighs. "Both, Firecracker. We're going to use both."

"Promise?" I ask with a saucy grin.

He leans in and presses his lips to mine. "Promise." It's a one-word reply, but the conviction in his tone has me pushing at his chest.

"Go. Go. Get on the road. We have tongues to use." I wave him away. He stands to his full height and closes my door. I start my car and watch as he climbs in his truck and flashes his lights. I assume it's a signal to follow him. He has nothing to worry about. I intend to make sure he keeps his promise.

"I like what you've done with the place," I tell Archer as we walk through his house from the kitchen to the living room. The last time I was here, I didn't take the time to look around. It's an open-floor plan, something that more and more houses are doing these days. I happen to love the design. I think it makes even the smallest of houses look bigger.

"You mean the way I moved in?" he asks, the humor in his voice evident.

"Are you sure that you live here? Is this just your hookup pad or something? You all share it, right? The four remaining single Kincaid brothers? How did you handle it when it was all nine of you at once? This is what, a three-bedroom?" I'm barely holding onto my laughter at the surprised look on his face.

"This is my home," he says. His eyes bore into mine. "My brothers *and I*, we don't have a fuck pad, Firecracker. No, we don't share. I live here alone."

"How long have you lived here?"

"A few years."

"Do you have an aversion to decorations?" I tease.

"What? There's a couch, a loveseat, a TV and TV stand, end tables, a coffee table."

"But they're all bare. Where are the throw pillows? The throw over the back of the couch for when you get cold? Lamps? Candles? Copies of *Playboy*? It's so... plain." I mean, I'm not judging him. I live out of a suitcase most of the time, but a home, it should be your safe haven, a place where you can be unapologetically you. My mind drifts to my parents' home, and my heart constricts in my chest. If the day ever comes that I have a permanent home, that's how I want it to be.

He shrugs. "I don't need much. It's just me living here."

"It's a fairly new house."

"It is. New construction when I bought it." He pauses, gauging how much he wants to say. "I figured I'd let my girl take care of all of that. I don't know dick about decorating."

"Your girl?" I croak out the words. "Do you have a girlfriend?" The words are out of my mouth before I can stop them. He's single. I've gotten that from multiple sources, but him talking about "my girl" has my anxiety spiking. I never want to be the other woman.

"No. Relax." He reaches for me, pulling me into his arms. "I meant when I find her. When I find the woman who will share this place with me, she can do whatever she wants to the place. I don't care what she does as long as she's here with me."

"Archer." I pause to gather my emotions. "That's really sweet."

"I'm a sweet guy," he counters.

"That's really how you feel?"

"It is. I'm a 'what you see is what you get' kind of guy, Scarlett. I have nothing to hide. I'm single, but I don't plan to stay that way. I'm certain I'll find a woman to share my life with. Most of my brothers already have, and they found them in the most unlikely of ways. I'm sure my turn is coming."

"And you want that? Marriage, kids, to be tied down?" In my experience, other than my adoptive dad, men don't want to settle down.

"I don't look at it as being tied down. I'd be sharing my life with that person. My hopes, fears, and dreams with her. That's not being tied down, Firecracker. That's living."

I've never questioned the way I live my life after losing my adoptive mom a few years ago. She encouraged me. Both of my parents instilled in me to follow my dreams, and to me, dreams are easier if you chase them on your own. There is less heartache involved. However, in this moment, I see the appeal of sticking around for a long period of time. Maybe even forever. Archer Kincaid paints a pretty picture, but then again, that's the life he's living. I don't know his family well. I'm closest to Palmer, but they all seem to have one of those fairy-tale kinds of loves that seem too good to be true.

I've turned the conversation into heavy topics when that's not why I'm here. He doesn't need to endear himself to me. Not that I think that's what he's trying to do. I believe him when he says he's a 'what you see is what you get' kind of guy.

"Hey, Archer?"

"Yeah?" His arms are still around me, his hands resting on the small of my back. He smiles down at me, and there is a flutter in my chest. I ignore it. This night is not about that. I'm not here for flutters in my chest or hearts in my eyes. That's not who I am, and he knows that. I'm here for his tongue and, if I'm lucky, his cock with a repeat of our first night together.

He's single.

I'm single.

We have needs, and I hope that we're both about to have those needs fulfilled.

"You mentioned something about your tongue."

"Right." He smacks my ass and lifts me over his shoulder fireman style and marches me down the hall. He pushes open a bedroom door and tosses me gently on the bed. "I need you naked, Firecracker." He reaches over and turns on the bedside lamp.

"What about you?"

He tilts his head to the side. "I'll race you."

I slide off the bed and stand toe-to-toe with him. "What do I get if I win?"

"What do you want?" he asks, tucking a loose strand of hair behind my ear.

"This." Reaching out, I palm his cock through his jeans.

"And if I win?" he asks, his voice strained.

"What do you want?" I fire back at him.

He hooks a hand around my waist, pulling me close. He proceeds to slide his hand under my long-sleeve T-shirt and beneath my leggings. "This," he says huskily. He traces his fingers gently over my clit. It's a feather-soft caress, but the simple act still has me burning with desire.

"Okay."

"Okay." He nods. "On the count of three." He kisses one corner of my mouth. "One," he whispers. He moves to the other side of my mouth. "Two."

Before he can say three, I grip the hem of my shirt and pull it over my head.

"You're cheating," he says, quickly doing the same. We race to strip out of our clothes. I'm breathing heavily because, dammit, I want to win. My mouth is watering, thinking of taking him into my mouth.

"Done," we say at the same time.

He stares at me, eyes not blinking. I shift under his gaze when a smirk slants his lips. He moves to lie on the bed and motions for me to come to him. "Come here." His voice is soft, almost as if he was talking to a child, but I take no offense. It's sexy and endearing.

"You got me here." I place one leg on the bed and then the other, facing him as I sit back on my knees. "Now what are you going to do with me?"

"Turn to face the foot of the bed."

I do as he says, my heart thumping erratically in my chest.

"Now I need you to scoot back."

Again, I do as I'm told.

"Straddle my hips."

I turn to look at him over my shoulder. "Like this? Facing your feet?" He nods, and I don't know where he's going with this, but I do as he asks. Once I'm straddling him, he grips my hips and pulls me backward. I shriek in surprise. "Archer!"

"Lean over."

That's when it hits me where he's going with this. I don't know why I didn't think of this sooner. I guess I was so focused on his instructions, the sound of his deep rumbling voice, all those hard muscles and his hard cock on display that I was blinded by what he was aiming for.

"Give me that pussy."

Not needing to be told twice, I move my ass back, giving it a little shake. He smacks each cheek, and I cry out, not from pain but from desire. His lips press against my ass cheek, and I know I can't let him have all the fun.

Gripping his cock, I stroke him a few times as precum coats the tip. I use that to lubricate my hand for each stroke. Then I lean forward and suck him into my mouth. The taste of him explodes on my tongue, and I moan in satisfaction.

What is it about this man that turns me inside out?

His mouth latches onto my clit, and I moan while his cock is buried deep in my throat. His legs twitch, and he grunts. I'm assuming that means he likes what I'm doing, so I continue on, full steam ahead. I suck while stroking him with my hands. Over and over again, I take Archer to the back of my throat. When I feel my orgasm building, I know I'm going to have to stop, or I could injure him as I clamp my jaw shut.

"Archer." That's the only word I can seem to form.

"Give it to me, Scarlett. I want your pleasure, baby. Come all over my face."

As if his words are a button to my pleasure, I do exactly that. My release tears through me like a raging inferno. He doesn't stop until my body falls lax against him. With his big strong hands running up and down my back, soothing me, I want to just lie here and enjoy the moment, but I still have work to do. Lifting up, I take him back into my mouth, and I won't stop until he's tapping my ass, telling me he's about to come. Even then, I keep going, and when he calls out my name and his cum coats the back of my throat, I swallow every last drop. I don't release him from my mouth until his body relaxes.

"Come here." Somehow, he manages to turn me so that my cheek is on his chest. He wraps his big strong arms around me, and I can't ever remember a time when I felt more content and safe. It's been four years, since losing my mom, that I've felt safe like this.

Tears prick my eyes, but I blink them away. "Thank you," I whisper hoarsely.

"Never thank me for giving you pleasure, Scarlett. It's an honor."

"A good performance should always be acknowledged." I try to lighten my own mood.

"You staying?" he asks.

I look up at him. "Do you want me to stay?"

His answer is to reach for the cover and pull it over us.

"What about the light?"

"I don't want to move. I want you just like this."

I chuckle and move to turn off the lamp and find my way back to his chest. It doesn't take long for me to fall asleep, wrapped in the security of his arms.

Chapter 7

ARCHER

S HE'S BEAUTIFUL.

I've been lying here for over an hour holding Scarlett while she sleeps, watching her like a creeper. I can't ever recall a time in my life when I was content to just watch a woman sleep. Scarlett is unlike any woman I've ever met. She's spunky yet soft, and she's not afraid to ask for what she wants.

I expected her to be gone when I woke up this morning, but I was pleasantly surprised to find her head still resting on my chest. I don't think either of us moved all night. I'm shocked, really. I'm not used to sleeping next to someone. Not unless it's my niece Blakely when she spends the night with me. She likes to sleep in my big bed, and who am I to deny my first niece?

Her lids start to flutter, and she opens her eyes. Vivid green eyes, a color I've never seen before her, smile up at me. "Hey," she says in her raspy morning voice. It's sexy as hell.

"Morning." I smile and place a kiss on the top of her head.

"Were you watching me sleep?"

No point in lying. "Yep."

"Creep."

I tickle her sides, and she laughs while rolling away from me. "I have to pee." She stumbles out of bed and rushes to the en suite bathroom, grabbing my shirt off the floor as she goes.

I take the opportunity to stretch. My body is stiff from sleeping in the same position all night, but I wouldn't change it. In fact, I think I could get used to waking up next to someone. My older brothers are onto something.

"Feed me, Kincaid," Scarlett says as she steps out of the bathroom wearing the shirt I had on last night.

Damn, she looks sexy in my clothes.

"Yes, ma'am." Tossing off the covers, I climb out of bed much more gracefully than Scarlett did moments before me. "I'll meet you in the kitchen," I say as I pass by her. I smack my hand to her ass for good measure. She yelps in surprise.

"Payback's a bitch, Kincaid," she calls after me over my laughter. I shut myself inside and piss, brush my teeth, and forgo a shower to make my guest some breakfast.

"Bacon and eggs okay?" I ask her.

"Coffee."

I laugh. "I'll make you some coffee. Bacon and eggs?"

"What kind of eggs?"

"Scrambled or over easy."

"Toast?" she asks hopefully.

"Yep."

"Scrambled. With cheese." She grins.

"Coming right up." I move to the coffee machine and start a pot before I get to work making us breakfast.

"Do you cook for all of your overnight guests?" she asks, perching her sexy ass on a stool at my kitchen island.

"No. They don't stay over."

"Oh, did I break an Archer Kincaid rule?" she teases.

"Nah, I was hoping you'd be here when I woke up."

"I don't date," she blurts. "I know we kind of talked about this that first night, but I'm only here for a year. There is no point in getting attached to someone when I'm leaving town."

"I know." I nod. I do know that. It's not like I want to propose marriage to the woman, but I do like the time that we've spent together this far.

I think back to my brother Rushton, and his now wife, Crosby. They were in a similar situation. Crosby didn't want to get close to anyone because she was afraid her contract wouldn't get renewed at the elementary school. This, however, is different. We know that Scarlett is only here for a year. Less than that now, and she's been very open about her dreams of travel photography.

She's a free spirit. Wild in a sense, and I would never want to hold her back. That doesn't mean we can't enjoy each other while she's here. It's just sex. I'm not one to sleep around, so it would be nice to convince her that we do this while she's here. When we feel the urge, we call the other and vice versa. No strings, and no looking for someone to scratch the itch as it arises, if you know what I mean.

"I don't date, but I like sex."

I cough, not expecting her bold statement, but I should have. This is Scarlett, after all.

"I like sex too."

"I like sex with you." She grins.

"I like sex with you too." I plate up our breakfast and slide the dish in front of her before pouring us both a cup of coffee. "How do you take yours?" I ask her. This is the most bizarre conversation I've ever had over breakfast, and I grew up with eight brothers.

"Just black for me."

"That surprises me," I say, handing her a steaming cup before taking the stool next to hers.

"Why does it surprise you that I like my coffee black?" She tilts her head to the side as if she's trying to see inside my head and can't.

"I don't know. You're vibrant and spunky." I shrug. "I just assumed you'd take your coffee the same way."

"What exactly does spunky coffee look like?" She's teasing, barely containing her laughter. "It sounds a little kinky." She wags her eyebrows. "Or a little gross. That could go either way."

"Lots of sugar, and cream and flavors, maybe? I don't know. I just wasn't expecting you to say black."

"Well, we have something else in common." I raise my eyebrows, not sure what the other thing is that we have in common. She smirks. "We both like sex with each other, I might add, and black coffee."

"Yeah, Firecracker. I guess we do. Eat up."

She makes a production of tearing off a bite of her toast and chewing. We both scarf down our food in comfortable silence. There is not an ounce of awkwardness to sitting next to this woman and sharing a meal. I barely know her, but I know that I want to. I want to keep this up, this benefits thing, and just enjoy her while she's here. I just don't really know if that's something she'd be up for. I assume she is.

"That was delicious."

"You were just hungry." I stand and take our plates to the dishwasher.

"I'm not really much of a cook, so trust me. It was great."

"Is it that you don't know how or just don't enjoy it?" I ask as I wipe off the counter.

"I know how. I just don't do it."

"Got it. You don't like to cook."

"I didn't say that."

I toss the sponge into the sink and turn, resting my back against the counter. I cross my arms over my chest and wait for her to elaborate.

"You know, showing off all that arm porn isn't a way to get me to talk." She points at my arms.

"What are you talking about?"

"That." She motions toward my arms again. "You have to know what those things do to a woman. Hell, probably some men too."

"Enlighten me."

"Nah, I don't think your ego needs more inflating." She's smiling, so I know she's teasing.

"Start talking, Firecracker."

"My mom and me, we used to cook all the time. Now that she's gone, it's not something that holds my interest." Her voice wobbles, and I know that confession was hard for her.

I pushed her, and I shouldn't have. I could tell her that I'm sorry and that I'm sorry for her loss, but I'm guessing that won't do anything to ease her pain. Instead, I move to stand next to her and wrap my arms around her in a hug. She's stiff at first, but she eventually relaxes into my embrace and hugs me back. I don't let go, sensing that she needs this. We stand here for what feels like hours, but I'm sure it's less than a minute when she pulls back and grins up at me, wiping her eyes.

"You give the best hugs." She smiles through her pain.

"Yeah? That was kind of our thing growing up. Nine rowdy boys and Dad, and then there was Mom. It didn't take long for most of us to be taller than her, and when she was emotional, or aunt flow was visiting, we didn't really know what to say or do, so we just gave her lots of hugs."

"Aunt flow? Really, Archer?" She giggles. I want to beat on my chest in the satisfaction that I brought her out of her sadness.

"What else am I supposed to call it? Guys don't talk about periods."

"You just did."

"Well, yeah, now we do. As teenagers, we were either grossed out by it or laughing about having to say it. Looking back, I feel bad for Mom. I'm glad my brothers are bringing their wives and more babies into the family. She deserves some females on her side for once."

"The aunt flow comment aside, I think it's sweet that you and your brothers tried to comfort her with hugs. It's endearing."

"Shh, don't tell anyone." I pretend to zip my lips, and her laughter rings out, filling the kitchen.

"Your secret is safe with me. I should get going." She stands and hugs me again. "Thanks for everything, Archer." She turns and heads down the hall toward my bedroom, and I find myself following along behind her.

"We should do this again." I nod to the bed.

She smirks. "Maybe."

"You've got my number," I tell her. I'm not going to beg her. I'm not a man who needs to beg for sex. I might not indulge as much as I could, but that doesn't mean that the option isn't there.

"And you've got mine."

I nod and watch as she gathers the rest of her things, slipping out of my shirt and back into hers. I should probably turn around or leave the room, but I don't know if this is the last time I'll get the chance to see her like this, and I'm a smart man. She's not shying away from me watching her, and I can't seem to turn away.

She steps toward me, and I offer her my hand when she gets close. I don't know why I do it. We're not together, and this wasn't a date. Maybe it was the conversation in the kitchen, and even though her eyes are clear of sadness now, I still remember it being there. "I'll walk you out," I finally say as she places her hand in mine.

Together we head down the hall, to the front door, and down the steps to where her car is parked in the driveway next to my truck. "I guess I didn't think about leaving my car here for everyone to drive by and see."

"You embarrassed of me, Firecracker?" I ask her.

"No. I just thought this is your town, and everyone knows you. I thought you might be embarrassed by me."

"Never." There is solid conviction in my tone. "I wanted you to stay. My life. My house. My business." I stare at her until she nods, letting me know she understands. I could never be embarrassed that a beautiful woman like Scarlett wanted to spend her time with me.

She rises on her tiptoes and presses a kiss to my cheek. "I'll see you around, Archer Kincaid." She turns on her heel and pulls open her car door. I stand here shirtless, in nothing but a pair of basketball shorts, and watch her leave. She waves as she pulls out of the driveway, and I return the gesture.

I stand here in the chilly April morning air and stare after her long past when her car is no longer in sight. Shaking out of my trance, I jog back to the house, already wondering how soon is too soon to call her and have her come back over. I know it's too soon, at least for a casual fling, and that's what this is. Even though my house now feels empty without her in it.

A few hours later, I'm sitting on the couch, watching an old boxing match, when the front door opens. Tilting my head back, I watch as Ryder comes into the living room and plops down next to me.

"What's up?"

"Tired of sitting at home staring at the walls."

"So, what? You decided you'd rather stare at mine?"

"Yep."

"You good?"

He leans forward and rests his elbows on his knees as he buries his face in his hands. "I don't know. Yes. No. Maybe."

"Have you heard from her?"

"Not for a couple of weeks."

"What can I do?" I don't tell him he's better off forgetting about her. Nor do I tell him that Jordyn, his girlfriend who traveled overseas for an internship, will change her mind and come back.

I don't know what's going to happen with them. I know that when any of my brothers have fallen in love, they fall hard. They love hard, and I know that this is eating my little brother up inside. He loves her. He misses her.

"Nothing anyone can do."

There is a long beat of silence that hangs between us as I let him gather his thoughts, composure, or whatever it is he's doing.

"You hungry?" I finally ask.

"Yeah, I could eat."

"Pizza Town?"

"I'll drive." Ryder stands from the couch, and I follow suit. I turn off the lights, grab my phone and keys, and follow him out the door.

"What's everyone else getting into tonight?" I ask once we're seated at a booth.

"Mav and Mer went to Sage."

Sage Night Club is a pretty popular hangout. There's not much to do in our sleepy little town of Willow River, but just a short twenty-minute drive to Harris, and the possibilities open up.

"That's the usual," I comment.

"Yeah, and the others are with their families."

"Working on making them bigger, I'm sure." I chuckle to help lighten the mood.

"My money is on Brooks." Ryder laughs.

"Agreed. I was there early yesterday to hang with Remi to give them some time together. I took her for a walk."

"No wonder he was all chill last night."

We share a laugh because it's true.

"Fancy seeing you here," a feminine voice, one I immediately recognize, says.

I turn and smile when I see Scarlett standing next to our booth. "Scarlett." I bob my head in greeting.

"Are you two out causing trouble?" She glances between Ryder and me.

"Nope." Ryder flashes her a grin. "Just feeding our bellies. We're growing boys, you know."

Scarlett laughs at that, and I'm unable to look away from her. "What about you?" I ask once her laughter has died down.

"Oh, just out exploring. I've not spent a lot of time in Harris. I went to a cute bookstore that Alyssa was telling me about and did some shopping. Now, I'm going to order some food to take home."

"You should join us," Ryder offers before I get the chance to.

I'm relieved because I know my request would sound way too eager.

"I don't want to impose."

"Not at all," Ryder says.

I move over, leaving room for her to sit next to me on my side of the booth. "No reason for you to eat alone when you can eat with us," I tell her.

"Are you sure?" She directs the question to Ryder, and I have to bite down on my cheek to hide my smile. She knows *I* don't mind her company.

"Yep. We're used to having lots of people around. Trust me."

Scarlett nods and slides into the booth next to me. "We haven't ordered yet," I tell her.

"Oh, I'll eat anything. Well, except anchovies." She shudders.

"Yeah, that's not happening," Ryder agrees.

We talk about what we're getting and decide on meat lovers and breadsticks. The waitress comes to take our order, and Scarlett jumps in, starting the conversation.

"So, I feel as though I'm at a disadvantage. You all know me and what I do. What do you do?"

"I'm a lineman," Ryder explains.

"Oh, so when my power goes out, you're the guy to call?"

"Not exactly, but yeah, I'd be the one out in the field getting you back up."

"Nice." She grins and then turns to me. "What about you?"

I take a drink of my sweet tea. "I'm a mason. I lay brick and block for a living."

"Nice. Explains the arm porn."

"What?" Ryder sputters with laughter.

"Arm porn," Scarlett repeats. "All of you have it in spades."

Ryder looks at me for help. "Apparently it's biceps."

"And you know this how?" he asks, still laughing.

"Scarlett and I have already had this conversation." I glance over at her, and she's nodding.

"It's a thing."

"I'll take your word for it," Ryder tells her.

Just like that, conversation flows. We each talk about our work, and Scarlett tells us about photography, and before we know it, we've devoured our pizza and breadsticks, and it's time to head out. We all have to work tomorrow, much to our dismay. We say our goodbyes, and Scarlett drives off in her Subaru while Ryder and I head back to my place in his truck.

I'm grateful that he doesn't mention my familiarity with Scarlett. I know he noticed, but he's giving me a free pass tonight. I make a mental note to do the same for him when he needs it. It's not often we give passes in our family. We're a loud, nosy bunch, but I always know at the end of the day, my family will be there whenever I need them.

Chapter 8

SCARLETT

"IT ONLY TOOK US A month, but here we are." Palmer raises her drink in her hand. "Here's to girls' night." We all clink our glasses together, even Crosby and Ramsey, though theirs is club soda.

"Why did it take us so long to do this?" Alyssa asks.

"Because we have needy husbands and their adorable offspring to take care of." Kennedy smiles.

"Their daddies are pretty damn adorable too." A dreamy look appears in Jade's eyes.

"Cheers to that." Palmer holds her drink up again, and we all do the same.

"So, Scarlett, how are you liking Willow River?" Ramsey asks.

"Better than I expected," I confess. "I'm a bit of a wanderer, so staying in one place usually grates on my nerves, but that hasn't happened here."

"How does your family feel about you traveling?" Piper asks. She's Palmer and Deacon's sister, and her little girl, Penelope, is an adorable little angel from the pictures she was showing earlier. I vaguely remember her and her husband from the wedding a couple of months ago.

"It's just me." I swallow a hefty drink of my beer. I hate this part. The part where I see pity in someone's eyes when I confess that I'm all alone.

"Well..." Crosby leans forward so that she can see around Alyssa. "It's a good thing you landed in Willow River. This place has a way of wrapping you in its embrace. The people aren't too shabby either."

Tension leaves my shoulders. They don't pity me. If they do, they're doing a great job at hiding it. I just want to be normal. I don't want to be the adopted girl who got a family only to lose them and be alone again. My mind goes to the stack of letters my mother left for me. They have specific scenarios of when I can read them. That was her way of staying with me, but she's always in my heart. She and my father both are. The first two people in my life who chose to love me.

The table erupts with laughter. "Let me call Rush and tell him you said he's not too shabby," Ramsey teases.

"He's already knocked her up." Jade grins.

"It's just me too," Crosby tells me. "I grew up in foster care. I applied for a teaching position here in Willow River, and well, here I am." She gives me a kind smile.

"It wasn't quite that easy." Alyssa jokes.

"No," Crosby agrees. "But the end result is still the same. I fell in love with the town and the people in it."

"I was in foster care, too, but I was too little to remember it. I was one of the lucky ones who were adopted." I take a sip of my drink. "I lost both of my adopted parents, and I was an only child, so were they. What extended family they did have, they weren't close to." I shrug as if the thought of being utterly alone in the world doesn't bother me, and most of the time, it doesn't. However, I'm going to be here for a little over nine more months. It's best to get the story out with these ladies so we can move forward.

"Are you single?" Ramsey asks, changing the subject, and I offer her a grateful smile.

"Yeah." I chuckle. "It's hard to get attached when you travel so often, never putting down roots."

"You know, we have some single brothers-in-law." Kennedy grins. "We could hook you up."

"Not really looking for anything serious," I tell them.

"A woman has needs." Piper grins, wagging her eyebrows.

"She has to pick." This comes from Ramsey.

"What?"

"You have to pick. It's kind of our thing."

"Pick what?"

"One of the single Kincaid brothers," Alyssa chimes in.

"English, please." I shake my head. I think I know what they're saying, but I'm going to need that to be spelled out for me.

"We've all done it," Jade explains. "Although the pickings are slim, and before you say Ryder, you need to know that he's involved... kind of. It's complicated."

"So that leaves Archer, Maverick, and Merrick. We're just going to leave Ryder off the list," Piper says.

"What about you? You didn't marry a Kincaid brother."

Piper shakes her head. "No, but I did have to pick, and Heath was my pick." She grins.

"So, who's it going to be?" Palmer asks me. She's wearing a wide smile.

With a quick glance around the table, I see they're all smiling and waiting with anticipation. I'm pretty sure they would lose their minds if they knew I'd already chosen and that Archer and I had already hooked up.

Twice.

Speaking of Archer, I should call him. In fact, I've wanted to, but I didn't want to come off too needy, so I've been holding off. Once a month is sufficient. I've gone months before him. As in over a year, but it's different when you know a sex god with arm porn for days is just a phone call or text message away from rocking your world or letting you rock his. I'm pretty damn sure it doesn't matter to either of us who takes control as long as we both get off.

"We're getting old here," Kennedy teases.

"You're really going to make me pick?" I ask them. I'm stalling. We all know it. I can't quickly say Archer and have them get romantic notions in their head.

"I'm not picking," I tell them.

"Oh, she wants them all." Crosby nods her approval.

"Stop." I insist. "That's not why I'm not choosing. I'm not sticking around. Willow River is a stop for me, and there is no point in any of you getting your hopes up that I might one day be changing my last name to Kincaid."

"I guess we can pick for you," Alyssa muses.

"We could," Palmer agrees. "But we'd have to make it interesting."

"Tell me more," Ramsey says, sipping her club soda.

"A contest, maybe?" Kennedy suggests.

"Yes!" Piper says way too loud, and I'm sure gaining the attention of the other patrons at the Tavern. She points her index finger at Kennedy. "I like how you think."

"This is going to be good," Jade adds.

"What's going to be good?" a deep, masculine voice asks.

I turn to look to see Jade's husband, Orrin, standing behind her at the table, with his hands on her shoulders.

"Babe, it's girls' night," she reminds him.

"And you all know damn good and well that we were going to crash. It's what we do. We gave you time to yourselves." He bends and places his lips on the top of her head. "We're over there." He points to a table. Collectively we all turn our heads, and sure enough, there is a table full of sexy men who raise their beers and smile at us.

"Did you draw the short straw?" Piper asks him. "They didn't want us to yell that we didn't get more time?"

"Nah, we were done with the new deck steps over at the twins', so we decided to have a drink."

"Have you talked to your parents? How are they doing with all the kids?" Jade asks him.

"Mom and Dad are in seventh heaven. They did say they wish Remi could be there." Orrin laughs.

"They have their hands full with two infants and Blakely," Palmer chimes in. "Besides, Mom and Dad were happy to take the girls. One for each of them."

"We keep having babies. We're going to need to get some more babysitters on staff." Orrin grins down at his wife.

"Don't let your parents hear you say that," Kennedy scolds him.

Orrin holds up his hands and starts to back away. "One beer for each of us, so you ladies do your thing." He winks and turns his back to us. He hasn't even taken a full step when Palmer calls out to him.

"Orrin."

He immediately turns and gives his sister-in-law his full attention. "We're going to need Archer, Maverick, and Merrick."

"What?"

"Just tell them to come over here."

"What do you have planned, Palmer?" There's suspicion in his tone.

"You'll see." She waves him off.

Orrin makes eye contact with his wife, and she nods, also waving him off toward his brothers. "Make room, ladies. Whatever it is that's about to happen, we're not going to miss it." He turns and saunters over to the table his brothers are sitting at.

It takes mere minutes for tables to be shoved together and for seats to be moved around as girls' night turns into whatever this is. Somehow all the husbands end up next to their wives, and they're immediately touching some part of them. Orrin has his arm on the back of Jade's chair, running small circles over her shoulder. Brooks pulled Palmer into his lap. Declan moved in close so that Kennedy could relax against him with the way they have their chairs positioned. Sterling took a page out of his older brother's book and pulled Alyssa onto his lap while Rushton laced his fingers with Crosby's and placed their joined hands on her slight baby bump. Heath, Piper's husband, also has his arm around her chair, only he's holding her close. Their chairs aren't even a breath apart. Deacon is sitting close to Ramsey with his hand splayed across her still-flat belly.

Ryder, Archer, Merrick, and Maverick just fill in the open spots, which leaves me sandwiched between the twins and sitting directly across the table from Archer. I don't look at him. I'm not sure how he feels about his family knowing that we hooked up. I don't care if they know, but I don't know him well enough to tell if he'll care.

"Look at you, a lovely Kincaid sandwich." Maverick leans in close and puts his arm around my shoulders.

"Double the pleasure." Merrick winks, and I can't help it. I burst into laughter.

My outburst gains the attention of the entire table, including a scowling Archer. "You two are ridiculous," I tell them. Merrick places his arm over Maverick's, and I do feel like I'm in the middle of a Kincaid sandwich.

"All right, boys." Ramsey sits up straighter. "I have a challenge for you."

"Oh, truth or dare?" Merrick asks.

"Something like that." Ramsey smirks. "We asked Scarlett here to choose, and she won't, so we're going to choose for her."

"Choose?" Deacon asks his wife.

Ramsey rolls her eyes. "We know you all know." She glances around the table at the men in her family. "We talk, you all talk." She shrugs.

"I thought the pick had to be just between the ladies?" Brooks asks, confirming that the guys do know.

"Yeah, isn't this sacred or something?" Sterling adds.

"It was," Palmer agrees. "But we're running out of eligible Kincaid men. We're down to three." She winks at Ryder, and he gives her a small smile in return with a slight nod.

"This is how it's going to go." Ramsey rubs her hands together.

"Babe, maybe we should stay out of it," Deacon tells his wife.

She waves him off. "We're family. We meddle. That's what we do." She smacks a kiss on his cheek. "Okay, so since Scarlett here won't pick, we're going to. We being the ladies."

"Hey!" Declan protests. "I want a vote."

"Ladies only," Kennedy tells her husband.

"Right. So, Maverick, Merrick, and Archer, you all have to kiss our girl here."

"I like this game." Maverick drops his arms from around my shoulders and sits up straighter in his chair.

"You're okay with this?" I ask Maverick.

"Have you seen you? Yeah, I'm good with it. Mer?" He leans around me to look at his twin.

"Don't fall in love with me, Scarlett." Merrick winks.

My face flushes, not because I'm at risk of falling in love with either of them, but because I said those exact words to their brother before we hooked up for the first time. It's not just a line either. I'm leaving. Willow River isn't my home. The last thing I want to do is leave a broken heart behind when I drive out of town.

"You have nothing to worry about," I tell him.

"You don't have to do this," Archer says. His voice is calm and quiet, but the look in his eyes tells me he's not impressed with this... choosing system or whatever you want to call it.

I shrug. "It's just a kiss. Or three." I smile, glancing from him to the twins, then my eyes go to Ryder.

He holds up his hands. "She's not here in this town or in this bar, but she's here." He places his hand over his heart.

I nod. "She's a lucky girl." I'm not just spewing sweet words. To know that he's that devoted to his girl speaks volumes for the kind of man he is. I don't know the entire story, but something tells me it's more than complicated.

"Right, so, who's going first?" Alyssa asks.

"Me," Maverick and Merrick say at the same time, both raising their hands.

"Is that a freaky twin thing?" I ask, laughing at them.

"That's a 'you're hot as hell' thing," Maverick answers.

"Merrick, Maverick, then Archer," Crosby suggests. "Since that's how the seating works out."

"Done." Merrick turns to face me. "You ready?"

I turn to look at Ramsey, ignoring Archer and the way his bulging arms are crossed over his chest as he glares at his younger brother. "Just a kiss?"

"Yep. We'll gauge the chemistry and decide for you."

I nod and turn back to Merrick. "Do your worst," I tell him.

He gives me a wicked, sexy grin and leans in, pressing his lips to mine. It's a chaste kiss as far as kisses go. He doesn't even try to slip his tongue past my lips. He pulls back and winks. I'm not sure what to make of that, knowing the kiss was bland as far as kisses go.

"My turn," Maverick says before I have a chance to try and decipher my interaction with Merrick. "Now, be prepared to be wowed," he says before leaning in and kissing me. He presses his lips to mine, similar to his twin. Maverick's kiss lasts a little longer, but it's still tame at best. He pulls back, a boyish grin lighting up his face. He turns to look at Archer across the table. "Think you can top that, big bro?" he taunts.

Archer pushes back from the table. The sound of his chair legs scraping against the old hardwood floor echoes throughout the bar. Even with all the background noise, it still sounds almost like nails scraping against a chalkboard.

My eyes follow him as he stalks around the table. It's not until he's standing behind my chair that I pull my gaze from his and look around the table. All eyes are on us, and I know I'm not going to be able to hide my familiarity with him. I'm usually pretty good at pretending, but this man, this mountain of a man, the gentle giant that is Archer Kincaid, I can't seem to hide how he affects me.

I feel his strong hands on my shoulders. He kneads the skin gently as if I'm his to touch freely. Tilting my head back, I smile at him. "I'm a sure thing, Kincaid." His eyes darken, and I realize my words have a double meaning. At least to him. "I mean, you're my last kiss, right?" I'm quick to add. I drop my head and stare straight ahead at where he used to be sitting. My palms are sweating, and my heart feels like it's about to thump right out of my chest.

What is this? I don't get nervous with men. Am I nervous? Is it anticipation? I think maybe a little of both. I know what it's like to kiss this man, and my body remembers. I crave him.

"Stand up, Firecracker." His deep voice is gravelly and so damn sexy.

The room fades away. All I can see is him. I think I hear someone ask about "firecracker," but I can't seem to focus on the words that are muffled. All I can see is him. Before I know what's happening, Archer is pulling my chair away from the table.

My legs are shaking as I stand, and I offer him a wobbly smile as I peer up at him. One large hand slides beneath my hair, cupping the back of my neck, while the other grips my waist. My body hums with electric energy that passes between us.

"Do your worst, Popeye." I drop his nickname. It's a whisper, but I know his family is riveted to the show we're putting on and won't miss it.

No further words are exchanged as Archer dips his head and kisses me. At first, I think his big production was just to prove he affects me, but his tongue traces my lips, and I open for him, letting him take control, and he doesn't disappoint. His tongue invades my mouth, and I savor the feel of his tongue sliding against mine. This has to be the hottest kiss of my life. I don't know if it's the audience or the way he has zero fucks to give as to the fact his family has a front row seat to him fucking my mouth. Whatever the case, my panties are ruined, and my poor heart is beating so fast I'm not sure it will ever recover.

I get lost in him. In the feel of his possessive hold on me. My mind can think of nothing but this man and the way he makes me feel. That is until I hear catcalls, whistles, and clapping. Archer pulls his lips from mine, and we both groan at the loss of contact. He then presses his forehead against mine.

"Didn't like seeing you kiss my brothers," he whispers.

"It meant nothing." Not like the kiss he just gave me, but that's not what we're about. That's not what I'm about, so I keep my mouth shut. I don't want to say something in the heat of the moment that will hurt him and me in the end.

Placing my hands against his chest, I push back, putting some much-needed distance between us. A hand appears in front of me, and it's Merrick. He offers me a bottle of beer, and I grab it, taking a long pull. I need to quench this desire. I need to rid myself of the taste of him.

Archer Kincaid just kissed the hell out of me.

That kiss... his kisses could change the world. I can't help but wonder if he's going to change mine.

Chapter 9

ARCHER

MY CHEST IS HEAVING WITH each breath that I pull into my lungs. My hands fall to my sides, and I clench my fists to keep from reaching for her. The thought of my brothers kissing her set my blood on fire, but witnessing it did something to me. Emotions I can't name, don't want to name, coursed through my veins, watching their lips on hers.

Thankfully, they both only gave her chaste kisses. It's as if they knew that I had her first. Yeah, I'm aware that makes me sound like an asshole, but I can't seem to find it inside me to give a flying fuck. Scarlett and I might only be sleeping together, but I don't share. Even though it's casual, I've shared enough in my life with eight brothers.

I don't share women.

Ever.

I'm not about to start now.

"Hey, Scar," Palmer says. Her voice is low and a little wobbly. "I think you chose just fine on your own."

The table full of my brothers and their wives murmur their agreement.

"It's the arm porn." Scarlett shrugs, and the table once again falls into a fit of laughter.

"Hey, are you saying we don't have sexy arms?" Maverick flexes his muscles. "Show them yours, Mer," he tells his twin.

I stand with my hands still fisted at my sides, my breathing starting to slow as I watch my two youngest brothers flex their muscles as if they're about to appear on TV for a WWE competition.

"I mean, that's impressive," Scarlett tells each of them. She even reaches out and squeezes each of their biceps, which has me grinding my teeth. "But this guy, he must eat his daily spinach." She turns to look at me, and the mischief in her smile has me relaxing my fists.

"Pft," Maverick scoffs.

"Go ahead, Arch, show us the guns," Orrin calls out.

I shake my head and playfully roll my eyes. "I don't need to flex," I tell him, my eyes staying on Scarlett.

"I mean, you could," she says, a light shade of pink coating her cheeks. "It would be a shame to deprive these lovely ladies and the rest of the Willow Tavern of seeing it." She glances over her shoulder. "I'm sure you've seen it, but I think we need a display." She turns back to face me. "I mean, your brothers showed me theirs." She smirks because she knows that she has me.

"They're my sisters," I counter, crossing my arms over my chest.

Scarlett takes a step toward me and pokes my bicep. "Then do it for me," she says softly.

"On one condition."

"What's that?" Her green eyes are filled with the same look she has when I'm thrusting inside her.

"You come home with me tonight."

"I don't know, Popeye. I'm pretty tired. It's been a long week."

I shrug. "That's the deal."

She sobers a little. "I really am exhausted, Archer."

"Then you stay and sleep with me. In my bed. In my house. Those are my terms." I don't know what the fuck I'm doing, but I keep seeing my little brothers kiss her, and I need something to focus on. I need time with her to erase the scene from my head.

"You want me to come home with you so I can sleep?"

"Yep."

"No funny business?" she asks.

She's surprised, and so am I. We're not dating. Hell, I'm not even trying to date her. I just know I don't want to walk out of this damn bar without knowing I get more time with her tonight. "Nope."

"Don't give me lines and empty promises, Kincaid."

"Never. I told you already. What you see is what you get. I have no reason to lie to you."

"Fine. But if you go back on your word, you have to shave your head," she blurts out.

I shrug. "I won't. You can place any kind of ridiculous stunt on me for breaking my word that you want. It doesn't matter because it's not going to happen tonight." I make sure I add that on there because I don't know what tomorrow will hold.

I also know that it's going to be hard as hell to lie next to her and not be buried balls deep inside her, but I gave her my word, and a man has nothing if he doesn't have his word. I fight a grin. My dad would be proud of that last thought.

"Fine. I'll come home with you. Now, give us ladies a show."

I smirk down at her as I lift my arms and flex. Whoops and hollers from our table greet me, and even a few not at our table. Willow River is a small town, and I know everyone here. They all know I'm not one to show off unless there's a gorgeous redhead taunting me to do so.

Scarlett licks her lips before turning to my sisters-in-law. "I need a drink."

The ladies agree, and before I know it, the bartender on staff tonight is bringing shots to the table for the ladies. Crosby and Ramsey pour orange juice into shot glasses so that the ladies can all toast together. That shot sets the tone for the rest of the night.

I sit at the table with my brothers, Deacon, and Heath, as we watch the ladies dancing and drinking. At first, I tried not to be obvious about watching Scarlett, but I should have known that eventually, one of my brothers was going to bring up the kiss.

"So, Popeye?" Rushton asks.

I shake my head. "Some ridiculous name she came up with because of the size of my biceps. She actually asked me if I ate a lot of spinach." Of course, she was kidding, but that shit's still funny.

"You too seem... close," Orrin says.

"We met at the wedding." It's not a lie, but not the complete truth either. I don't know why I don't just spill the beans. We all know I will, well, not the intimate details, but as brothers, we don't really keep secrets. Brooks tried, and we still found out about him and Palmer. It worked out for them. Scarlett, she's not sticking around, so their meddling and the meddling of their wives is unnecessary.

"Bro, come on, that was not a first kiss." Sterling gives me a pointed look.

"Since when do we kiss and tell?" I ask him.

"We don't if it's a forever kind of thing."

"Scarlett is a free spirit. Wild. She's not about to get tied to a small town like Willow River." She's told me enough that she's not staying so I know it to be true. We're just having fun. That's all this is.

"So there is something there?" Brooks prompts.

"We've hung out a couple of times."

"Be careful, Arch. She's not sticking around." Ryder's voice holds a touch of sadness.

I wish we knew why Jordyn left. Even more so, I wish my brother wasn't hanging in limbo, waiting on the woman he gave his heart to to come back to Georgia. He's hurting. He misses her, and it's tough to watch. We've always been there for each other, quick to help solve issues, but this one, it's not something we can help with. Ryder and Jordyn will have to figure it out on their own. I just hope that she comes home, and they can either work things out or get the closure that I know he needs.

"Just hanging out, Ry," I tell him.

"So, that wasn't your first kiss?" Declan inquires.

"Nope."

"And that possessive hold you had on her?" Heath, Piper's husband, asks.

"You were seeing things."

"Nah," Maverick says. "We're all seeing fine. It's you who's not seeing things clearly."

I turn to my little brother and glare at him. He just shrugs.

"Mav's right," Merrick adds. "We all saw not only the hold you had on her but the look in your eyes. Never seen you look at a woman like that."

"Ramsey said she signed a one-year contract to work for Palmer and then plans to leave," Deacon says.

I raise a curious brow, and he laughs. "I listen when my wife talks."

"She'll be here a little less than a year. Nine months or so, I guess now."

They don't tell me to be careful. They don't have to. Ryder is the only one who speaks about it, but I know the others are thinking about it. The Kincaid men don't fall often, but when we do, we fall hard. I know this about the men in my family, but I've got this on lockdown. Two consenting adults enjoying each other's company.

Will I miss her when she's gone? Yeah, I'm sure I will. She's a cool chick. Gorgeous and unlike anyone I've ever met. Will my heart be broken? Not likely. I understand their concern. "I've got this," I tell them. "This is no different than anyone else I've hung out with."

"Yeah, keep telling yourself that." Brooks chuckles.

I don't get a chance to reply because the ladies are making their way back to our table. "I'm all danced out," Ramsey tells Deacon.

"We're out," he says, standing and wrapping my cousin in his arms. His hand goes to her belly. It's still flat, but after watching Orrin, Brooks, Declan, and even Rushton with their pregnant wives, I know he doesn't care that you can't see the evidence of her pregnancy. They know it's there.

One by one, each of my brothers stands to collect their wives. I stand as well, stretching my arms above my head, and my eyes land on Scarlett. She's wasted. The glassy look in her eyes and the cheesy smile on her face are a dead giveaway. Her eyes land where my shirt has risen just above my waistband, and she licks her lips.

I remind myself that she's off limits, at least for tonight, as I push my chair in and make my way around the table to where she's standing. "You ready to go?"

"Shh," she says dramatically, holding her index finger to her lips. "They might hear you."

"They know that wasn't our first kiss, Firecracker."

"Huh," she says and leans into me.

I wrap my arms around her, holding her close. "Where are your keys?" I ask.

"In my purse."

"Here you go." Crosby hands me said purse. "You're taking care of her, right?" she asks.

"I've got her."

"Okay." Crosby leans in and hugs us both. "Be safe. It was nice to have you join us tonight, Scarlett. We try to do this once a month or so when time allows. I'll make sure Palmer lets you know."

"That. Do that." Scarlett nods vigorously, making us laugh.

"She's three sheets to the wind," I tell Crosby and Rushton, who comes to stand next to his wife.

"Take care of her." There is something in my sister-in-law's voice that has me quickly reassuring them that I've got Scarlett covered. Crosby didn't have the best upbringing, and I assume she and Scarlett bonded over that fact. I'm sure that Crosby sees a little of herself in Scarlett.

"Come here." Despite my brother's protest, I pull his wife into a hug. "I promise she's safe." Crosby nods against my chest before stepping back, letting her body relax into Rushton.

"Well, see you guys later." With Scarlett's purse in one hand and my other wrapped around her waist, we reach my truck, and I lift her into the passenger seat. "Can you buckle yourself in?"

"I can, but what if I want you to do it for me?"

With a soft laugh and a shake of my head, I lean into the truck and secure her seat belt. Just as I'm getting her belt locked into place, I feel her hands in my hair. When our eyes meet, I see the same hunger I feel for her staring back at me.

"Why are you taking care of me?"

Her question catches me off guard. "Because you need me."

"Just that simple?" she asks softly.

"Yeah, Firecracker. It's just that simple." Not able to resist, I press my lips to the corner of her mouth before pulling away and closing her door behind me.

I slide behind the wheel and glance over. She has her eyes closed and her head tilted to the side. She looks so peaceful, and even with the glow of the parking lot lights, she's the most gorgeous woman I've ever laid eyes on.

"I've got you," I whisper as I lift Scarlett into my arms. She immediately locks her arms around my neck and holds on tight.

"Archer?"

"It's me," I tell her.

"Where are we?"

"My place. You said you'd come home with me, remember?"

"Are we going to have sex?" Her voice is sleepy and sexy. Add her question to that dangerous combination and my cock rises to the occasion.

"Not tonight."

"I have to win a bet."

"You have to sleep."

"I'm pretty tired."

"I know you are, Firecracker." I carefully take the steps to my front door, knowing I have precious cargo in my arms. I somehow manage to get the door open without putting her down or dropping her and make my way inside.

"I'm going to put you down."

"No. I like it when you hold me."

Damn. "I'll be right back. I promise. I have to go lock up the house. I left the door open." I don't know why I'm explaining it to her. She's half passed out.

"You said you don't break promises."

Laying her on the bed, I quickly turn on the bedside lamp before kneeling next to her, pushing her hair out of her eyes. "I don't, baby." The term of endearment just slips out, but I don't panic. The chances of her remembering any of this tomorrow are slim.

"I'm going to lock up so you're safe inside, and then I'll be right back."

"I'm always alone."

My heart cracks right in two at her whispered, sleepy confession. "Not tonight, Scar. Tonight, I'm right here." Standing, I lean over the bed and drop a kiss on her forehead before hustling out of the room to shut and lock the front door. I make a quick detour to the kitchen to grab a bottle of headache medicine from the cabinet and a couple of bottles of water from the refrigerator. I need to get her to drink at least one of them before she's out for the rest of the night and swallow a couple of these pills to help prevent her hangover in the morning.

"Fuck," I mutter when I step into the room. I was gone three minutes tops, and she managed to strip herself naked to nothing but a pair of panties. No, those aren't even panties. They're just a thin strip of fabric that barely covers her pussy, let alone her ass. I swallow hard before stepping into the room.

As quietly as I can, I place the waters and the medicine on the nightstand and move across the room to grab her a shirt to sleep in. When I turn back, I take a minute to memorize her naked in my bed. It's not the first time, but I still want to stop and remember it. I know it's wrong, but it's nothing I've not seen before. Nothing she hasn't shared with me in the past, and besides, she's the one who stripped naked.

Moving toward the bed, I manage to help her sit up and get her dressed in one of my shirts. "I need you to take some medicine and drink some water for me."

"You came back."

"I told you that I would."

"I'm not alone."

"No, gorgeous, you're not alone." Grabbing a bottle of water, I screw off the top and take a drink so it's not so full that we spill it everywhere and help her take small sips until over half of the bottle is empty. "Good girl. I need you to do one more thing for me." I shake two tablets into my hand and help her take them before settling her back into bed and pulling the covers over her. I reach up and turn out the light, and she gasps.

"Archer?"

"I'm right here." I move in close and am able to offer her my hand in the darkness. "I'm just going to change and go to my side of the bed." It's technically all my side since I'm the only one who sleeps here, but that's the easiest way I can explain to her that I'm not leaving.

"Okay." Her voice is soft and timid, and I can't help but wonder if it's more than just losing her parents that put the sadness there. I know a little about her life, from foster care at a young age to losing both of her adoptive parents. It's heartbreaking, and the worry accompanied by the wobble in her voice grips my heart like a vise.

I manage to strip down to my boxer briefs and slide into bed beside her in record speed. I waste no time pulling her into my arms. I promised her she wasn't alone, and I need for her to feel that. It's more than just knowing that I'm here. I need her to be able to listen to my heartbeat as she sleeps against my chest. I need her to feel my arms wrapped around her in a warm embrace.

She settles into me, and I close my eyes, listening to her breathing. I'm drifting off to sleep when I hear her say, "Popeye always saves the day."

I grin and kiss the top of her head, holding her just a little tighter.

Chapter 10

SCARLETT

I FINISH WRITING BLAKELY'S NAME on the card and slide it inside the sparkling pink gift bag. I've met Blakely a few times since arriving in Willow River, and she's a vibrant little girl. When Kennedy came into the studio and insisted I come to her birthday party this weekend, I couldn't say no. Furthermore, I didn't want to say no.

It has nothing to do with knowing that I'll get the chance to see Archer. He took care of me and kept his promise after girls' night. I expected him to try and seduce me, not that it would have taken much the next morning, but he was the perfect gentleman. He made me breakfast and drove me home. I haven't seen him since. Trust me, every single time I'm out and about in town, my eyes are scanning, looking for him.

Gathering my purse, keys, phone, and Blakely's gift, I lock up the house and head out to my car. I'm leaving earlier than I need to. The GPS on my phone says it's only a twenty-minute drive to the address Kennedy gave me in Harris, where the party is being held, but I don't know where I'm going, and I hate to be late.

The drive is nice. There's not a ton of traffic from Willow River to Harris, which I'm thankful for. I crank up the radio and sing my heart out. The sunroof is open, and the sun is shining. There's nothing better than a bright sun shining day, the radio cranked, and the sunroof open. The scenario never fails to put me in a good mood, and yeah, it turns me into a rock star. I chuckle to myself as I follow my GPS, which instructs me to turn left into a large parking lot of an even larger building with a giant LED light sign that reads Karting Express.

"Only Blakely Kincaid," I say to myself. That little girl marches to the beat of her own drum, and I love it. I love that Declan and Kennedy let her be who she is. I don't know many little girls who would want to have a princess birthday party at a go-kart track.

Grabbing everything I need, I climb out of the car and make my way inside. I see the huge party room off to the right, and there is a dry-erase board on the window wishing Blakely Kincaid a happy birthday. Looks like that's where I'm headed. Pushing open the glass doors, I step inside the room.

"Hey," I greet Kennedy.

"Scarlett, hi." She waves.

"Can I help with anything?" I ask, placing the gift bag on the table where a few gifts are already sitting.

"I think we're all set up. They're making the pizzas. We're going to eat, ride go-karts, have cake, open presents, and probably more go-karts. We rented the room for the entire day," she explains. "With my husband and his brothers, it was necessary. They love this place."

"Big kids at heart," I reply.

"You have no idea." She laughs. "I was just situating the cupcakes and cake. Everything else was already set up when we got here."

"That makes it nice."

"It does, but there are so many of us even when we get together at one of our houses. It doesn't take long to set up or take down with everyone pitching in."

"Mom!" Blakely comes barging into the room. "Uncle Ryder beat Daddy!" Her excitement is contagious.

There are four little girls who trailed in after Blakely and look just as excited that Declan lost. "High five." I raise my hands to Blakely first and then to each of her friends as we celebrate Ryder's win.

"That's what I like to see," a male voice says. I look up to see Ryder. He grins and moves straight for Blakely. I watch as he lifts her into his arms and swings her around in a circle. Her laughter rings around the room, her friends cheering and asking for a turn.

Ryder places Blakely back on her feet, making sure she's steady before moving on to each of her friends. The giggles of all four girls fill the room.

"You want a turn?" a deep voice says from behind me. I know it's Archer. I can smell him. Sandalwood and something uniquely him. It could also be the way he rests his hand on my hip and squeezes gently before releasing me. It's as if my body knows his touch.

"If I were six, I'd say yes."

"What? You think I can't lift you in the air over my head and spin you around?" He seems to be stunned that I would think that.

"I'm not fun sized like they are." I nod toward the group of girls.

"Is that a challenge, Firecracker?"

"Is what a challenge?" Ryder asks.

"Scarlett here seems to think I'm not capable of lifting her in the air and swinging her around like you did those little ladies." He winks at the girls, and the room once again fills with giggles.

Even at five and six, these girls know that the attention of a Kincaid man is something to celebrate.

Ryder smirks. "What, you think that arm porn is just for show?"

"I... don't know," I confess.

"What's for show?" Maverick asks.

I turn to look over my shoulder, and somehow the room is now filled with Kincaids. I'm usually more perceptive, but Archer has a way of sucking my attention along with all of the air in the room.

"Are we putting on a show?" Merrick asks. He glances over at his niece and her friends with his brow furrowed.

"No. Scarlett is challenging Archer," Ryder speaks up.

"No. No. No. That's not what's happening here."

"Oh, I think it is. You're not backing out now. Are you, Firecracker?"

"I didn't say that either." I'm stuck between a rock and a hard place here. I don't want to show off at Blakely's party. This is her day, but dammit, I don't like to back down from a challenge either.

"What's the challenge?" Declan asks.

"Scarlett doesn't think I can spin her around like Ryder did with the girls."

"I've got twenty on Arch," Sterling says.

"We are not placing bets," Alyssa scolds her husband. She turns to look at me. "But if we were, I'd put my money on Archer too." She winks at me, and I can't help it. I laugh.

"Fine. If you want to show off your arm porn and the skills it took you to get it, who am I to stop you?" I stand up tall and square my shoulders. I know that in about two seconds, he's going to have his hands on me, propelling me into the air, and I have to seem unaffected. It's not that I don't think that he can do it. It's more that my self-preservation was hoping he would back down.

They all know that he took me home from the Tavern two weeks ago, and now here we are. They want to know. Palmer has been giving me side-eyes and smirks since then, but I pretend to ignore her every time she does. He took me home. Well, the next day. I probably won't tell them that he took care of me and held me in his arms all night. No, I won't ever tell them that. I also won't tell them that he brings me a sense of security that I've been missing for far too long.

I'm not thinking about that.

I'm not talking about that.

Pretend.

Deny.

That's my grand plan. "Are we doing this?" I ask. I'm pretending to be annoyed when I'm anything but.

Archer smirks as he steps in close. His toes are touching mine as he places his hands on my hips and peers down at me. "We're doing this," he says huskily. His tone tells me he's talking about more than just twirling me in the air.

Swallowing hard, I nod. Archer's grip tightens, and then I'm being lifted into the air. He lifts me straight up. His arms are fully extended as he holds me high above his head. I look down at him to find that he's already looking up at me. I grip his forearms, not sure when the twirling is going to start.

"I've got you, Firecracker." His voice is soft, his words only for me, as he slowly turns in a circle, never taking his eyes off mine.

He makes two complete rotations. At least, that's what it feels like from my vantage point. Maybe there were more? Honestly, I can't be sure. I know we're in a room full of his family at his six-year-old niece's birthday party, but at this moment, it feels as if it's just the two of us.

Lost in our own little world.

He never pulls his eyes from mine as he lowers his arms. My body slides along the length of his as he settles me back on my feet. He slides his arms around my waist, and it's on pure instinct that I snuggle into his chest.

I've forgotten where we are.

I've forgotten that we have an audience.

Archer bends his head and presses his lips to the top of mine. "You good, Firecracker?"

It takes great effort, but I manage to lift my head and look up at him. I open my mouth to reply, not sure exactly what I'm going to say, but a loud whistle pulls me out of my trance.

"Damn." I turn to see Merrick with a paper plate fanning his face. "That was hot."

"Definite *Dirty Dancing* vibes," Maverick agrees. He holds up his own paper plate with a nine scrawled on it in crayon. "I had to deduct a point because we needed the kiss." He winks, and my face heats.

I Immediately step away from Archer, missing the heat of his body pressed to mine. I chance a quick glance at him, and he's glaring at his little brother. I need to defuse the situation.

"Meh, I'd give it a seven at best."

"What?" Archer chokes out a laugh.

I shrug. "I expected the full twirling experience, Popeye. It's okay. I know you don't have the strength for that. Apparently, that arm porn of yours is deceiving."

I don't have time to run when he leaps toward me and lifts me into the air. This time he spins me around just as Ryder did the girls. I squeal with laughter and, for a fleeting moment, hope that I don't end up crashing into someone as he spins us in a circle.

By the time we stop spinning, I'm laughing so hard my entire body is shaking from it. Archer places me back on my feet, and I stumble.

"Solid ten!" Maverick and Merrick shout.

"Ten. Ten. Ten," the girls chant.

I look up at Archer, and he's not even breathing heavily from the act of spinning a full-grown human in the air. "I guess you ate your spinach this morning," I tease.

"Yuck," Blakely says. "I don't like that. It's icky."

Her friends agree with her. "Spinach will make you big and strong like Uncle Archer," I tell the girls.

Blakely shrugs. "All my uncles are strong, and I don't need to be. I have them."

"The birthday girl has spoken." Archer scoops Blakely into his arms and plants kisses all over her face. She laughs and tries to wiggle out of his hold, but as she said, he's too strong for that, and she's, well, not.

"All right, kiddo," Declan calls out. "It's time to eat. You girls are over here." He points to a small round table that's already set up with a plate filled with pizza, along with cups with straws and lids for the girls.

Turning my back on Archer, I walk to where Kennedy is standing. "What can I do?" I ask her.

"Well, if you want to take Beckham, I can make sure the girls have everything they need."

"Done. Come here, handsome." I take the adorable baby boy into my arms and snuggle him to my chest. He's sleeping through all of the chaos that's filled the room. I move to a small table in the back corner and pull out a chair, sitting gingerly so that I don't wake him up.

"He likes you."

I look up in time to see Crosby take the seat next to mine. "I think this little angel just likes to be held." I smile at her.

"Oh, for sure, but that's not who I was talking about."

I don't ask her who she's talking about because, after our little show a minute ago, there could only be one other *"he"* that she's referring to. "We're friends."

She nods. "They're a great family. I'm really lucky that they've pulled me into their orbit."

"I'm pretty sure Rushton wouldn't allow them not to," I tell her. I've seen the two of them and how they respond to each other. You can see the love they have for one another with a quick glance when they're together, hell, in the same room as each other.

"You're right." She nods. "I know they can be overwhelming, but don't let them scare you away."

"I'm just here for my contract," I remind her.

"You know, my story and yours, they're rather similar."

I nod. "Our backgrounds."

"All of it. I had to take a contract here in Willow River to teach for a year. I immediately fell in love with the town and the people in it. I just didn't know if my contract would be renewed."

"See, you wanted to stay. My heart is on the road."

"You sure about that?"

I give her my full attention. "Yes?" It comes out like a question, and she chuckles softly.

"Are you asking me or telling me, Scarlett?"

"Telling you. Photography was always my thing. I was kind of a loner. No, I was a loner growing up. Trust doesn't come easy for me. I spent a lot of time hiking with my parents and fell in love with the landscape. It's what I've always wanted to do."

"I've seen your work. The images from the wedding were amazing."

"Is that your way of telling me that I can do something different?"

She points at me. "Beauty and brains."

I shake my head and smile. "One day, maybe. I'm not saying I'll never put down roots, but the loss of the life that I was gifted when I was adopted is still too fresh. Too raw to settle in any kind of life without them." I feel myself start to get choked up.

"I understand that too. Trust me. If there is anyone here who understands, it's me. I didn't get the adoptive parents, but I can imagine how having that and losing it after losing so much before them would hit hard."

I nod.

"However, think about them for a minute. They were your parents. DNA aside, they chose you. They chose to love you and give you a life so many of us were not so lucky to have."

"I know." I swallow hard and turn my gaze to the sleeping baby in my arms. I don't know the history of my birth parents. All I know is that they willingly signed their rights to me away.

"They would want you to be happy, Scarlett." She holds up her hand when I start to speak. "I'm not saying that you're not. I'm also not saying that chasing your dream across the globe isn't what's going to give you that feeling of rightness that we all seek. What I am saying is that they wouldn't want you to close off your mind or your heart to love. They'd want you to find a love like I'm sure they had. They'd want to know they have grandbabies and that their family history lives on through you."

"Are you trying to make me cry?" I ask, my voice cracking.

"No." She smiles. "Just telling you that I've been where you are. The difference was that I knew I wanted to stay. I knew this was where my heart was. I just wasn't sure I could grab onto everything I wanted, everything that was right in front of me. I was too scared to risk the pain to me or to Rush, and in the end, it worked out. However, had I not gotten that contract extension, I think I would have stayed. My heart and his were already too invested for me not to."

"You would have given up what you'd worked so hard for?"

She nods. "Yeah, I would have. This family, there's this dynamic. They're loud and nosy, and they love so hard. It was more than just Rushton that I would have been leaving, and that was too large of a loss. I would have figured it out. Kept applying to local schools and started my own tutoring business... something. I would have made it happen." She chuckles. "It sounds so easy now," she tells me. "When I was living it, that's a different story. I was stressing over how I felt for him and my contract and being able to stay. They say that in life, things tend to work themselves out, and I agree, but I know when you're close to it, it's hard to look at things from that perspective."

"Archer and I are just friends," I tell her again.

"Yeah, I was friends with a Kincaid man once too." She rubs her small baby bump. "It changed me. Changed my life." She leans her shoulder into mine. "If you get to that point"—she gives me a look that tells me she's certain that I will—"I'm in your corner. I'm here for whatever you need."

I start to tell her that it's not going to happen, but I can see it in her eyes. It doesn't matter what I say, she's team Kincaid—as she should be—but she won't believe anything I say on the matter. That's okay. She'll see that my situation might be similar, but it's oh so different.

"Thank you, Crosby."

"You want me to take him?" I startle as Archer stands over me, pointing to his nephew.

"No. He's good where he is."

"I'll make you a plate," he says, and he's gone just as quickly as he appeared.

Crosby's smile tells me everything she wants to say. Thankfully, she keeps her words of wisdom or her predictions to herself. "What would you like to drink?" she asks, standing.

"Oh, I'll grab a bottle of water in a little while."

"I'll have Archer bring you one." She walks to where Archer is making two plates. He nods and then reaches into one of the coolers and grabs two bottles of water before heading in my direction.

"You sure you don't want me to take him?"

"No. He's fine."

"Here." He sets my plate in front of me and opens my bottle of water, making sure I can reach everything with my free hand before he takes a seat next to me at the small table and starts to eat.

Everything about the scene is domestic, and there's a tightening in my chest.

Maybe one day I'll have this. Maybe one day, I'll get over my fear of losing someone else I love and allow myself more than just my career.

Chapter 11

ARCHER

I'M SITTING IN THE PARTY room at Karting Express, watching as my niece opens her birthday presents. She's laughing and smiling and every single present is her favorite. This kid, she's so full of love and of life. We all spoiled the hell out of her while she was the only niece, and even now, we continue to do so.

"That's for all your secrets," one of her little friends explains as Blakely opens a small pink journal with a pen with feathers to match. "My sister writes all hers, but she also tells them to her best friend when she's on the phone," the little girl rambles.

"I don't have secrets," Blakely tells her. "But I like to draw."

"My sister says that your uncles are hotties." The same little girl giggles.

"Oh, yeah?" Maverick asks.

I roll my eyes and chuckle at the same time. My little brother is all about the ladies. Both of the twins are. It's going to be fun watching them fall for the one woman who turns their world upside down.

My eyes dart to Scarlett. She's now holding Remi, bouncing her on her hip, making her laugh. They're both smiling, and it's stunning.

She's stunning.

All five of the girls cover their mouths with their hands to hide their giggles. I swear one of them, the one who is telling her big sister's secrets, is blushing. I think her name is Isla. She's a cute kid, but I'm sure her sister would be pissed that she's giving the room a tell-all of her life.

"Tell your sister Maverick said hi." Mav winks at the girl, and she nods her little head up and down so fast she looks like one of those bobbleheads.

"All my uncles are hotties," Blakely tells her friend. "That's 'cause they gots the arm porn." She smiles up at Kennedy, who's standing with a shocked expression on her face. "Daddy too, right, Mommy? That's whys they kiss so much." Blakely's voice is calm as if she was discussing the weather.

"Blakely." Kennedy manages to say. It's a half gasp, half scold. Clearly her daughter has shocked her. Hell, she's shocked all of us, but I don't know why. The things this kid says, she's her own person, that's for sure.

"What do you know about arm... that?" Declan asks his daughter. His voice is gritty, as if saying the words pains him. I'm sure it does. Isn't it illegal for a six-year-old to say the word porn?

"Daddy." Blakely sighs as if having to explain is exhausting her. "That's your muscles. That's how Uncle Archer and Uncle Ryder could lift us. But Uncle Archer's arm porn is bigger porn, so that's why he lifted Scarlett."

I choke on a laugh, as do the rest of the adults in the room. Declan kneels next to his daughter. He looks up at his wife, and she gives him a crooked smile. One that says it's a tough job, but somebody has to do it, and I'm glad it's you. I've seen that same smile pass between my parents too many times to count. It's half smile, half grimace. For a new mom, Kennedy has perfected it. I guess she didn't really have a choice with Blakely as her daughter. I can't imagine how feisty she's going to be as a teenager.

"Baby girl, that's a word that only grown-ups should say."

"Why?" She tilts her head to the side. "Is it a curse word?"

"No, but it's still a word that only adults should use. You can't go around saying... what you said," he stumbles.

"Fine, but we're adding that word to the bad word list. My piggy bank is hungry, Daddy."

"Deal." Declan gives her a one-armed hug and kisses her cheek before standing and moving toward his wife.

"I'm so sorry." I hear Scarlett tell them. "This is my fault."

"Nah." Declan gives her a kind smile. "She's a sponge, and if I told you some of the things that kid comes up with, you'd know this is normal Blakely. She keeps us on her toes."

"Oh, you mean her wiener pants?" Kennedy laughs.

"What?" Scarlett looks stunned.

"Remind me to fill you in another time," Kennedy tells her. "My list of things Blakely says is ever growing."

"Besides," Brooks speaks up, taking Remi from Scarlett's arms, "we've all taught her bad words." He shrugs. "We had to learn to clean up our act when she was born." He tickles Remi's belly, and she giggles. "I'm certain this little one is going to be the same way. It's hard not to be when she has all these uncles around. It's not a big deal," he assures her.

"I'll do better." Scarlett has so much conviction in her voice that anyone would believe her.

"Mommy, can we ride go-karts?" Blakely asks as she stands and pushes all of her new gifts to the side of the table.

"Sure, sweetie. You have to wait on us to come with you."

"I'll grab an uncle," Blakely tells her mom. She reaches for Sterling's hand and begins to lead him to the door. "Come on. Let's race!" she says excitedly.

"You need four more," Kennedy calls after her.

"Why four more?" Scarlett asks.

"They're not tall enough to ride on their own. They have to be in a kart with an adult. We debated on having the party here, but we figured we have enough adults or man-children that we could make it work," Kennedy explains.

"What can I do to help?" Scarlett asks.

"Actually," Palmer speaks up, "do you mind taking this?" She holds her camera that's hanging around her neck up in the air. "I need to get this one down for her nap, and I don't want to miss this."

"Absolutely." Scarlett's eyes light up at the possibility of having a camera in her hands. "Anything particular you want me to capture?"

"Everything," Kennedy and Palmer say at the same time.

Kennedy chuckles. "We love pictures, and there are a lot of us, so we like to spread them out among us. We're kind of spoiled having a professional photographer in the family, and now we have two." She winks at Scarlett, and I'd give anything to know what that shared look between them means, and since when is Kennedy saying that Scarlett is a part of our family? Sure, we're a big group, and we'd gladly bring her into the fold, but there's something inside me, something I've never felt before. Something that's screaming that if Scarlett is a part of this family, she'll be mine.

She's not mine.

I need to keep reminding myself of that.

The lines are starting to blur.

I'm very aware that I'm the one blurring them. I never realized that it would be this incredibly difficult to resist the temptation that is Scarlett Hatfield. She's this addictive little spitfire that I can't stop thinking about.

"Go, Blake!" I call out to her. She's riding with Ryder, and they're currently in the lead. Her little hands are gripping her steering wheel, which does nothing to steer the cart, but by the determined look on her face, you would think that it does.

"Look at this one." Scarlett, who is standing next to me at the fence, leans over and shows me the back of Palmer's camera that she's using. "Look at her grin."

"She loves this," I tell her. I try not to stare at Scarlett like a creeper, even though I want to. I could watch her for hours. I might have made it a point to stand back and see where she ended up to get the best shots just so I could stand next to her.

I just need one more time with her, and I'll have her out of my system. Sex with Scarlett is the best of my life. That has to be what this is.

"I can see that. The way she likes pink, I was surprised this is where her party was held."

"She's a tomboy who loves pink and loves dolls and makeup. She was raised by ten men and my mom. Well, Alyssa was around a lot, too, but mostly men. We did the best we could."

"You all did a fantastic job. She's a happy, well-adjusted little girl." She pauses. "Where was Kennedy?"

"Kennedy isn't Blake's biological mom."

"Oh, I didn't realize. You would never know."

I nod. "She loves her just as much as she does Beckham. They might not share DNA, but they are mother and daughter."

"If there is anyone who can understand that, it's me. Well, Crosby, too, I suspect."

Declan, Ryder, Deacon, Brooks, and Sterling all bring the go-karts to a stop in the line. The girls are all smiles as they wait for help from the attendant to unstrap their safety belts so they can climb out.

"Can we do that again?" one of them asks.

"We can," Declan tells her. "But the adults are going to go next."

"Come on, girls," Alyssa calls out. "Let's go take a potty break."

"I'll come too," Crosby tells her.

"Aunt Crosby Kincaid is having a baby. Aunt Alyssa is too. They can't ride," Blakely tells her friends.

"Just Crosby or Aunt Crosby, sweetheart." Crosby smiles at Blakely.

"What's the story there?" Scarlett asks.

"Crosby was—is her kindergarten teacher. She was Miss Crosby Greene to Blake, and then she went and married her uncle. It's a habit that's hard for her to break since they are still in school for another week. She still has to call her Miss Crosby or Miss Kincaid. She'll get it," I say with confidence.

"That's the sweetest," Scarlett announces.

I peer down at her, and I'd love to kiss that smile on her lips. "How about you give that back to Palmer"—I nod to where my sister-in-law is sitting with a now-sleeping Remi beside her in a stroller—"and race me?"

"Oh, honey, are you sure you're ready for that kind of embarrassment?" she fires back.

I lean in close, feeling her hot breath as it fans across my face. "Bring it, Firecracker."

"Don't say I didn't warn you." She turns on her heel and marches over to where Palmer is sitting. She hands her the camera, and the two share a laugh that I'm sure is at my expense. Not that I care.

She waves to Palmer and moves to get in line for a kart. I shake my head and follow along after her like a puppy.

I'm in the middle of an internal debate on whether or not I should let her win when Jade slides up beside me.

"You racing?" I ask her.

"Yeah, we all are." She nods to where all of my sisters-in-law and even Piper are headed toward us. I scan the room and see Alyssa with Palmer's camera sitting on the table in front of her. She has Beckham in her arms, and Remi is sleeping in the stroller. Crosby is holding Penelope, Piper's daughter, while she pushes a stroller that Orion is sleeping in back and forth with her foot, and they both seem to be keeping an eye on Blakely and her friends as they make their way through what I know to be thirty dollars in quarters that Declan brought for the arcade today.

"They're fine," Jade assures me. "They can handle it."

"I know. You all could. You're like super moms or something," I tell her.

She laughs. "It helps when you have a huge support system."

"I don't think that pizza is sitting well with me," Piper says from behind us.

I turn to face her. "You okay?"

She waves me off. "Yeah, but I think I'm going to sit this one out." She steps out of line and heads to where Crosby and Alyssa are sitting. She latches on to the stroller that Orion is sleeping in and begins to push him around.

"Is she pregnant again?" I ask Jade.

She chuckles. "I mean, it's possible. Penelope will be what, seven months old? She's a week younger than Orion."

"We're going to be covered up with babies, aren't we?" I ask her. Piper is Palmer's older sister and Ramsey's sister-in-law, so she might not be married to one of us, but she's still family, still connected, and we treat her as such.

"Probably."

"You plan on adding to that number anytime soon?" Jade asks me as we take a step forward when the line starts to move.

"Yeah, I mean, I don't know how soon. I need to find me a baby momma first."

"Are you looking?"

"I'm not *not* looking, if that makes sense."

"Surprisingly, yes, it does. Come on. It's time for me to show you boys how it's done." She starts weaving through the line, that's all family, to get to the front faster.

"Scarlett already promised to put on a clinic for us," I call after Jade.

Scarlett, who is standing at the front of the line, holds her hand up to Jade for a high five. "You know it, Kincaid!" she calls back to me.

I'd love nothing more than to march up to her and kiss the sass right from her lips, but I've already given my family enough of a show for one day. Instead, I remain where I am, moving up with the line. When I reach the front, it's just Jade and me left to claim our karts. To my surprise, Scarlett and Palmer are in the last two karts in the back row.

Jade and I both take one in the middle and strap ourselves in. I fight the urge to look back at Scarlett, but I'll see her soon enough when I lap her on the track. I was considering letting her win, but that sassy mouth of hers changed my mind.

The light turns green, and we start to move. As soon as we clear the gate, I push the gas pedal to the floor. Deacon flies around me, laughing all the way. I shake my head at him and keep my foot down. I don't care how many of them pass me. Just as long as she doesn't pass me.

Damn, I should have made a bet with her. If I win, she will come home with me. If she wins, I go home with her. Yeah, that's a positive outcome either way, but I missed my opportunity.

Instead, I'm racing like this is the Daytona 500 and there are millions of dollars and a big ass trophy to hoist over my head in the winner's circle on the line.

I don't dare look back. Honestly, I don't know what place I'm in. Deacon passed me, but I zoomed past Orrin and Sterling. We're all spread out at random places on the track. I'm not sure any of us really knows who's in the lead. What I do know is that the lovely Scarlett has yet to pass me, so to me, I'm still winning.

I grip the wheel as we come to a sharp curve. Just as we are about to go around it, a kart in front of me spins out. It's Maverick. He's laughing, as are the rest of my brothers. I grin and slow down to keep from hitting him.

"Later, suckers!" Scarlett waves her hand in the air as a few wisps of her red hair flies behind her. Palmer is right on her tail, and they're wearing matching smiles. I wait for the disappointment to settle inside my gut, but her smile prevents that from happening.

Scarlett has been through so much in her life, and she still manages to find joy in everything she does. Not that I'm a depressed guy, and I've had a good life. A great life. I'd like to think I'm happy and easy to get along with. However, there is something infectious about Scarlett and how she views things. She's definitely a "glass half full" kind of person.

Instead of using the final laps to try and catch her, I goof off with my brothers. We start weaving in and out and back and forth with each other, just being silly, and it reminds me of when we were kids. We were always doing this kind of thing. Get all nine of us on the track and we dominated.

Just like we are tonight.

We're not dominating the race, but we are dominating the track. Putting on a show for anyone who might be observing. Part of me wishes that Scarlett was standing at the gate watching, but the other part is glad that she's out here.

Living.

Smiling.

The light turns yellow, and we're instructed to slowly make our way back to the main entrance. Once we're parked and given the go-ahead to unbuckle, I'm out of my cart and looking for her. She's standing with Palmer, Kennedy, and Jade. They're all laughing and passing out high fives. She fits in so well with them, as if she's always been a part of our lives.

"Oh, Archer, the loser's lounge is that way." Scarlett points to a small sitting area of couches through the glass doors.

It's a room where people can sit and watch and not be out here with the smell of all the fumes and be sheltered from the loud noise of the race.

I open my mouth to smart off but decide better of it. Instead, I bend and lift her over my shoulder. She shrieks as I carry her out of the race area and back to the party room. When I place her on her feet, she stumbles, but I'm there to catch her at the same time I kiss the hell out of her.

She fists my shirt, and I taste her for the first time in far too long. We're hidden in a back corner, so when I hear the door open, I ease out of the kiss and step away from her.

"Uncle Arch! It's time for cake!" Blakely comes barreling into me, and I lift her into my arms.

"You know I love me some cake," I tell my niece. My eyes find Scarlett's, and we share a look. One that is filled with heat and promises of more kisses. More… everything.

For the remainder of the day, I pretend like I don't want Scarlett. I pretend like her mere presence doesn't affect me. And when it's time to go home. I walk her to her car and say goodbye. I don't ask her to come home with me. I don't hint for her to invite me to hers. Instead, I do the right thing and put some well-needed distance between us. She's worming her way under my skin.

She warned me this might happen.

Chapter 12

SCARLETT

I SMILE WHEN I PULL the camera away and view the screen. I got the perfect shot of Rushton kissing Crosby's belly. Her face is lit up as she smiles down at her husband. The love that the two of them share bounces off the screen.

When Palmer asked me if I minded working today so she could help her mother-in-law and her sisters-in-law with Crosby's baby shower, I quickly agreed. She tried to offer to pay me, but I refused. It's not like I have a wild social life. Besides, I might not be a permanent resident of Willow River, but I'd like to think of Crosby and the rest of the ladies as friends or really good acquaintances, at the very least.

I went ahead and told her to pencil me in for Ramsey's shower in a few weeks as well. They're not combining the events because they said both new moms need to have their special day, and I happen to agree with them.

"Can I see?"

I know that voice. I don't even try to hide my smile as I turn to look at Archer. "I was wondering if you were ever going to come and say hi."

"This is for the ladies. We were outside manning the grill." He nods to the patio door where all the men who have ladies inside are sure enough congregated around the grill.

"All of you?" We both know it doesn't take all of them to man the grill. I just like to tease him.

He shrugs and nods to the camera. "Whatever you were looking at made your face light up."

"Oh." I turn the camera so he can see. Archer apparently doesn't think that's good enough. He steps in close, sliding his arm around my waist, as he leans over my shoulder to look at the back of my camera.

"Wow, Scar. You're really talented."

"Nah, you don't have to have talent when you have good subjects." I flip through a few more images slowly so he can see. Part of me wants to show off because I've gotten some really good shots, and the other part of me just wants to keep him close to me for a little longer.

"You got plans after this?" he asks.

He still has his arm around my waist, and he's looking at pictures as I move even slower to flip through them. To anyone watching, it looks like we're only looking at pictures.

"Nope. I'll probably go home and work on editing these so I can get them back to Crosby."

"Does that have to be done tonight?" he asks. His hot breath fans across my cheek, and it's taking everything I have not to show him how he's affecting me.

"No, it doesn't have to be done tonight," I finally answer.

"Come somewhere with me."

"Where are we going?" I don't know why I'm asking. I'm going to go no matter what he says we're doing. I've been craving time with him. Not just my body but my mind too. I've been stubborn and not willing to reach out because I like his company too much.

"I'm taking you fishing."

"Fishing?" I turn to glance at him over my shoulder. That puts our mouths just a breath apart, and I've never wanted to kiss someone so badly in my entire life. He's right there. I could just lean a little closer. Just a quick peck, a taste after weeks of nothing from him.

"Yeah, Firecracker. I want to take you fishing."

I swallow back my desire. "Why haven't you called me?" I ask, turning back to my camera. I keep my voice even, and I'm hoping he can't see the need in my eyes. This man... he's addicting.

Dangerous.

"Work has been brutal. We're on a job that's about an hour and a half away right now. We've been working long hours trying to wrap it up. We're supposed to be starting a new elementary school in Harris after this. They just got a grant approved."

"So you weren't avoiding me?" I ask, still flipping through the images. I'm pretty sure I'm already on my second run-through of all the ones I've taken today.

"No, Scar. I'm not avoiding you." He pauses. "I can't stop thinking about you." His lips press against my ear. "About the feel of your pussy choking my cock."

I cough and try to step away from him, but his hold on me is strong. "Archer," I hiss.

"You going fishing with me?"

"Is fishing code for... something?" I ask.

He smirks. "Only if you want it to be. But no, I was planning on going, just relaxing, and I also want to see you. Two birds, one stone."

"I've never been fishing."

"Really?" He grins. "Bring your camera. I have a feeling you're going to want it once you see where we're going."

"Done." There's no point in pretending like I don't want to go. "Where should I meet you?"

"I'll pick you up. I'll head to my place and load up what we need and then swing by yours."

"What do I need to bring?"

"Just you and your camera. I'll take care of everything else."

I smile at him. "I can't wait."

"Scarlett!" Kennedy calls. "Do you mind grabbing a few shots of the gift table before we start opening gifts?"

"Already done," I call back to her.

"Perfect. Let's do this."

Everyone gathers around Crosby, and their backs are to the rear of the room where I'm still standing with Archer. I lift my camera to take a picture from this vantage point when I feel his lips against my cheek.

"Until later, Firecracker," he says huskily. He lets his fingers trail across the expanse of my back before he walks away.

I stand frozen as I focus on getting my breathing under control. Desire and excitement courses through my veins. I've missed him. He didn't admit it, but I'm pretty sure fishing is a euphemism for sex, and if it's not, well, it's going to be after tonight.

All it took was a simple touch and the sound of his voice, and my panties are ruined. I curse the fact that there's still a couple of hours or so before this shower is over, and I'm just going to have to deal.

Crosby starts opening her gifts with her husband at her side. Rushton holds up an outfit to her baby bump, and everyone laughs at his antics. There's a pang of envy gripping my chest like a vise. This here is what I've always wanted. Maybe not right now, but someday. I've always wanted a husband and kids. I vowed at a young age that I would make sure my kids were loved and that they knew it. My parents gave me that when they adopted me. Sure, I'm still a little messed up about being abandoned by my biological parents, but we don't know the story, and we never will. That's something that I have to live with. I've been through thousands of dollars of money in therapy to be able to admit that to myself. It's not that I remember my time in foster care, but I know about it. There's just something about knowing that you weren't good enough for the two people who gave you life. Then again, I don't know the circumstances either. All the more reason it sometimes messes with my head.

Then I lost them. My parents. The ones who chose me. They chose to love me unconditionally. They were my first example of what love looks like. I always wanted what they had, but now they're gone. Once again I'm all alone. Left with nothing but the pain of their loss beside me as I venture through life.

I spend the next few hours hiding behind my camera. I might sneak a picture or two of Archer. Only a few are for me, and the rest will go to Crosby with the rest of the memories from today.

"Thank you so much, Scarlett," Crosby says, pulling me into a hug. "I cannot wait to see the pictures."

"I went a little crazy," I tell her.

"Perfect. I want all the memories." Her eyes shimmer with tears, and I pull her into another hug. I feel a connection with Crosby, with the two of us having a similar background.

"You're going to be the best mommy," I say softly, keeping my words low, just for her.

She pulls back, wiping at an errant tear. Her smile is wobbly, which has Rushton on high alert.

"Hey, you okay? Is it the baby?"

"I'm fine," she assures him. "Just happy."

"Love you." He kisses her temple, and her body relaxes into his.

"Do you need help with anything?" I ask.

"No. You've done so much already. I can't wait to see the images," Crosby says again.

"I'll have them to you next week. I'm going to head out. Thank you so much for allowing me to be a part of your special day."

"You're always welcome here," Crosby tells me. There's something in her eyes, but it's gone before I can decipher what she's trying to tell me.

I make my way around the room, saying goodbye to everyone before heading out to my car.

I'm barely at the end of their street when my cell phone rings. Reaching over, I dig it out of my purse, keeping my eyes on the road. As I pull up to the Stop sign, I see Archer's name, and my heart skips a beat.

"Hey," I answer, trying to sound as unaffected as possible.

"I just wanted to let you know that I'm leaving now too. I'm going to stop and get what we need. Give me twenty minutes or so to be at your place."

"Sounds good. You sure I don't need to bring anything?"

"I'm sure, Scar. I'll see you soon. Drive safe."

The call ends before I can tell him the same. Placing my phone in the cupholder, I continue on the short drive to the small house I'm renting in town. I was lucky to find it. Alyssa said she had a place she could have rented me. I guess Crosby rented it after she moved out, but I'd already committed for a year on the lease when I found out she had a place available.

By the time I'm pulling into my driveway, I've decided to pack some snacks. I rush into the house, knowing I don't have much time. The first thing I do is grab a second battery for my camera and a new SD card. Once that's in my camera bag, I rush through, changing into a pair of cutoff shorts and a tank top, and slip my feet into a pair of flip-flops.

I decide on peanut butter and jelly sandwiches because that's what I have, and this is last minute. I have one of those multi-packs of small bags of chips, so I toss a few bags into a reusable grocery bag, along with the package of Soft Batch cookies I picked up at the store earlier this week. They're my weakness, and sharing them with Archer will keep me from polishing off the entire pack while I'm editing the baby shower images later this weekend.

I add a couple of bottles of water to the bag and call it good. I'm hoping that Archer has a cooler, but if not, warm water is better than no water. As I lift the bag on my shoulder to head outside to wait for him, there's a knock at the door.

Quickly, I grab my camera bag and my purse and open the door. "Hey. That was fast."

He reaches out and takes my camera bag off my shoulder. "I had a good incentive," he says, reaching for the other bag. His tone is soft, almost sensual.

"I've got this one."

"What's in there?"

"I made us some snacks. Do you happen to have a cooler with you? That's something you take fishing, right?" I ask.

"Yeah, Firecracker. I have a cooler full of drinks."

"Good. I need to put all of this in there. You think there's room?"

"It'll fit."

"Perfect." I close my door, making sure it's locked, before bouncing down the steps toward his truck. "Keep up, Kincaid. We've got fish to catch."

"Yes, ma'am," he replies.

He meets me at the bed of his truck and helps me place everything in the cooler. "Snacks were a good idea. I was just going to stop at the gas station and see what we could find."

"Well, it's nothing fancy, just a couple of peanut butter and jellies."

"Perfect. Thank you for doing that." He closes the cooler and the tailgate of his truck. "You ready for this?"

"Yep. I have no idea what I'm about to get myself into, but I'm here for it."

"Let's go then." He walks me to the passenger side of the truck with his hand that sits on the small of my back, burning through the fabric of my tank top. Archer pulls the door open for me and waits until I have my seat belt fastened before shutting the door and rushing around to his side.

"So, where are you taking me?" I ask once we're on the road.

"Willow River."

"Aren't we already in Willow River?"

"The actual river, baby."

Baby. I pretend to ignore the way butterflies take flight with his use of the endearment. "Got ya. New girl here, remember?"

"Not so new," he says, reaching over and lacing his fingers with mine.

I don't resist because I'm starved for his touch. This is bad. Very bad. I know Archer is different. I'm not able to forget about him, and I have to. However, for tonight, I'm pushing my worry aside. I'm going to pretend like he's not working his way beneath the walls I thought I had carefully constructed around my heart.

Archer pulls his truck off on what appears to be an old dirt road. "Are we allowed back here?"

"Yeah. It's public, but few come back this far because they're leery of getting stuck."

"And we're not worried about that?"

"Nah, we're not worried about that."

He continues to drive until we come to a clearing. It's an open space that leads to the river. There are wildflowers everywhere, and my finger itches to capture the moment.

"I think you need this." I pull my gaze away from the beautiful setting to see Archer smiling from the driver's seat, holding my camera bag out to me.

"How did you know?"

"That goofy, happy smile on your face, and your finger was tapping."

I swallow hard that he knows me that well, or at least thinks he does. Who am I kidding? He nailed my mood, my thoughts, and my need for my camera. "Gimme." I reach for the bag and make quick work of switching out the SD card and changing the lens before pushing open the truck door. I turn to look at Archer over my shoulder. "Am I allowed to explore?"

"Yes. Just don't go too far. It's going to get dark soon."

"I just want to... yeah, I won't go where I can't see you." The words are barely out of my mouth before I jump out of the truck and snap pictures as I walk through the field of wildflowers. Archer's deep chuckle trails behind me.

When I reach the opposite side of the clearing, there's a small wall of rocks. It's perfect to climb up on and get a higher vantage point. I get lost in my love of photography. I take shot after shot. I even zoom in on Archer, who's sitting in a chair on the river bank with his fishing pole in his hand.

I don't know that I've ever had a man think about my passion. He didn't really want to go fishing. I know him well enough to know that. He knew I would fall in love with this place. I should be worried that he's making this "arrangement" of ours about more than just sex, but I can't be. Not right now. I love that he did this for me, and I have the sudden urge to show him. The sun is starting to set, and I snap a few more pictures. The lighting is incredible as the sun sets over the lake. These are shots that I'm certain I'm going to want to blow up and hang on my wall.

I'm in Willow River for several more months. I can make my rental more my own until then. I'm not much to brag about, but I'm certain these shots deserve to be displayed. Maybe I'll give Archer a copy too.

I make my way to where he's sitting on the bank. He looks up when he hears me. He's smiling. "Good time?" he asks.

"Yeah, Popeye." My voice is thick from the emotions welling up inside me. "Good time," I manage to reply.

"That's yours." He nods toward the empty chair. "You ready to fish?"

"Sure. I just need to get my camera bag."

"Here." He reaches beside him and grabs it from the top of the cooler. "I didn't want to set it on the ground, and I assumed you'd want it when you got back."

"Thank you."

He nods. "Now, are you willing to bait your own hook?"

"What exactly does that consist of?" I ask.

"Putting a worm on the hook."

I shrug. "I'll try it. No promises." He looks surprised but stands and grabs the extra pole and shows me what I need to do. "Ewww," I say, as I run the hook through the worm like he instructs. "That's not pleasant," I tell him. "And the poor little worm."

"You did great, Scar." He moves to stand behind me. "Okay, this is how you cast." He places his hands over mine, and we pretend to cast a few times so I can get the hang of the motion. Then he shows me what to do, and together we cast my line.

"Now what?" I ask, glancing over my shoulder at him.

"Now we wait." He moves to take his seat, and I do the same in the one he brought for me.

"This is so peaceful."

"Yeah."

The silence ebbs between us, but it's not uncomfortable. In fact, it's the most relaxed I've felt in years.

"You didn't really want to go fishing, did you?"

He turns to look at me and studies me for a few heartbeats. "I like fishing. It's been a while, but I just wanted to spend time with you. I thought you might like this place." He motions toward the field of flowers behind us.

"You were right." I turn my gaze back to the river, which really looks more like a really large lake. "The company's not so bad either," I confess.

Chapter 13

ARCHER

T HE SUN SET ABOUT THIRTY minutes ago, bathing us in darkness, with nothing but the moon and the stars to light our way. I hate that I can no longer see her beautiful green eyes, but that's okay. I know what they look like. I don't think I'll ever forget their emerald-green color.

"I thought the point of fishing was to actually catch the fish?" Scarlett asks.

I chuckle. "Somedays you have better luck than others."

"At least it's a nice night."

I turn to watch as she tilts her head back, peering up at the stars.

"Yeah," I agree.

"Is the water warm?" she asks.

"Yeah. This time of year it is."

"Are we allowed to swim in it?"

"Some do. Are you a good swimmer?" No way am I letting her go in at night if she's not, and she has to stay close to the shore. What am I saying? No, we're not going swimming tonight. I can't risk something happening to her.

"We should do it."

"Not tonight."

"What? Why?"

"We don't have suits." Not that that really matters. That's a better excuse than me admitting that I'm stressed about something happening to her in the dark water.

"Meh, who needs them." She stands and reels in her pole, setting it on the ground. I watch with rapt attention as she lifts her tank top over her head and tosses it onto her chair.

"Scarlett." There is a warning and question in my tone.

"Are you scared, Kincaid?"

"Yes." My confession shocks her. Her hands freeze where they are unbuttoning her shorts. "It's dark. You don't know the waters."

"No, but I have you." She gives me a bright smile and continues to unbutton her shorts and slide them over her hips.

"This isn't a good idea." I know that we're safe from prying eyes out here. I drove to the other side, opposite where people usually gather to fish or hang out. If someone heads our way, we'll be able to see and hear them long before they see us. I wanted some time just the two of us. I had hoped our night might end with me buried deep inside her, but never once did I think this was what she would want to do.

"We'll stay close to shore or the edge. Is it still the shore for a river?" she muses.

She knows the answer. She's just fucking with me. "How strong of a swimmer are you, Scar? Seriously. Stop for a minute."

She places her hands on her slender hips and tilts her head to the side to study me. She's in nothing but a white bra and panty set that seems to glow beneath the light of the night sky. "I took swim lessons for years. I've swam in the ocean more times than I can count. I'm a strong swimmer."

"There are fish and... other things." Fuck, I can't think with this woman standing in practically nothing.

"We're going to be fine, Archer. Now, are you joining me?" She reaches behind her back and unclasps her bra. My eyes are glued to her as she slides one strap and then the other over her shoulders before pulling it off completely, and it, too, gets tossed onto the chair.

"You're overdressed, Kincaid."

"Shit," I mutter, kicking off my shoes and stripping out of my shirt and shorts in quick succession.

"Is that for me?" she asks, walking toward me like the beautiful vixen that she is. She palms my cock in her hand and strokes me through my boxer briefs as I inwardly curse myself for leaving them on.

"It's not for the fish," I husk out.

She laughs, the sound echoing through the night air. "We're almost there," she says, dropping her hand. She takes a step back and bends at the waist, pulling her panties down her long legs. "Ready?"

"You stay next to me, Scarlett. I mean it." My heart is pounding. I'm not sure if it's from looking at her or if it's my anxiety about something happening to her. I'm pretty sure it's a combination of both.

"Yes, sir." She salutes me. Her tits shake with the action.

"Fuck it." I do quick work of getting rid of my boxer briefs and take one long stride to get to her. I bend and lift her over my shoulder. Her soft skin against mine feels incredible. I walk us to the side of the river and take a cautious step into the warm, night-covered water.

I don't stop until I'm waist-deep. I let Scarlett slide off my shoulder but keep her close, pulling her into my chest. "This was a good idea after all," I say, bending to press a kiss to her bare shoulder.

Scarlett wraps her arms around my neck and her legs around my waist. My cock pulses, begging to enter her.

"I knew that arm porn of yours would come in handy one day." She laughs.

"To hold you up in the water?" I ask.

She nods. "What about outside of the water? Do you think you could hold me like this without the water assisting you?"

"You didn't learn your lesson the last time you questioned my strength?"

She bites down on her bottom lip. I'm holding her wet, naked body in my arms. Leaning in, I trace her lips with my tongue before giving her a soft kiss.

"I know you're extra strong," she says dramatically. "But I don't know. I kind of had something in mind, and I don't know if you're up to it."

"If it's with you, I'm all in." The words are out before I can stop them or think better of what I'm saying. Oh, well, it's the truth. I crave time with her. It's been too long, and right now, she could ask me anything, and if it's within my power, I'd make it happen for her. That's a scary revelation, but I shake out of that train of thought and keep my mind on the beautiful woman in my arms.

I expect her to tell me what it is she needs me to do. What I don't expect is for her to hug me tightly and bury her face in my neck. Something coils and snaps loose inside my chest. I'm not supposed to like her as much as I do.

I'm in trouble.

I feel her lips press against my neck, and I plant my feet in the muddy bottom of the river to hold us steady. My toes dig into the muck, and my hands grip her ass tighter. That's not so I won't drop her. That's to keep from pushing my cock inside her. One quick thrust is all it would take.

She trails kisses up my neck to my cheek. When she reaches my ear, she whispers, "Can you fuck me like this? Holding me like this?"

I swallow hard and remind myself I'm a man, not a randy teenager. "Is that what you want?" My voice is gravelly, but that's not something I can control. I'm too turned on to care.

"You probably can't do it. That's okay. It was just an idea."

I growl. I'm pretty sure I've never growled like this before in my entire life, but there is no other way to explain the sound that rips from the back of my throat. My feet are moving, slicing through the dark water and taking us to the shore. My grip on her ass is tight as we emerge, water dripping from us.

"I thought you wanted to swim?"

"This sounds more fun." Her reply is breathless, and my cock weeps to be inside her.

I march to the truck, grabbing my T-shirt out of the chair along the way. I manage to hold on to her and lower the tailgate at the same time. I toss the T-shirt down as a barrier for her and place her on top of it. Then, I frame her face in my hands and kiss the breath from her lungs. Pushing my tongue past her lips, I explore her mouth like it's my fucking job to know every single inch of her inside and out.

"You're supposed to be holding me."

"Trust me, Firecracker. I understood the assignment." I press another quick kiss to her lips before stepping away from her.

"Where are you going?" she calls out. "You can't just leave me here all worked up like this, Kincaid."

I ignore her shouts as I stalk through the grass in my still mucky bare feet. When I reach the passenger door of the truck, I tear it open and fumble to reach inside the glove box. I stored a box of condoms there before I left the house today. I stopped on the way home from the shower and grabbed them. I was hopeful we would go back to her place or mine. If it was hers, I wanted to be prepared. I have another unopened box in my nightstand.

Grabbing the box, I tear it open and rip off what I need before slamming the door and stalking back to where I left Scarlett on my tailgate. I hold up the condom, and she grins. "Were you a boy scout?"

"No." I huff out a laugh. Tearing the condom open with my teeth, I quickly sheath my hard cock, tossing the wrapper on the tailgate. "Come here." I move in close, and Scarlett leaps into my arms. I steady my feet as her mouth fuses with mine.

"Now, Archer."

What the lady wants, the lady gets.

Keeping one arm wrapped around her, holding her close, I take the other and guide my cock inside her. She moans as she sinks down on me. She lifts and then falls back on my cock, and I grit my teeth.

She feels too fucking good.

I let her play, making sure she's nice and wet. "You ready for more?" I ask, trailing kisses down her neck.

"Everything, Popeye. Give me everything."

I grip her ass as I spread my feet apart, bracing myself. I lift her up and slam her back down on my cock. She moans a low, growly sound from deep in the back of her throat before she chants the word "Yes," over and over and over again.

"Is this what you wanted? Did you want to ride my cock?" I ask.

"Faster."

Fuck me. She's going to kill me. "My fucking pleasure," I answer, giving her exactly what she wants. With a punishing pace, I lift her up and down on my cock. Her nails dig into the back of my neck, and from the sounds she's emitting, she's enjoying herself immensely.

"Archer... I'm close. Oh... there. Right there," she instructs.

I don't slow down, giving her everything she needs. Her pussy starts to quiver around my cock, and I'm thankful as I'm ready to blow. I never would have thought that sex with Scarlett could get any better.

I was wrong.

Dead fucking wrong.

"Good girl, milk my cock." The words are barely out of my mouth before her orgasm crashes through her like a blazing inferno. I don't stop until I feel her pussy relax, and that's when I thrust twice. Two more hard strokes of her pussy on my cock, and I'm calling out her name as I still and bury my face into her neck.

We stand motionless, wrapped around one another in the dark of night. Nothing but the moon and the stars up above. The sound of crickets in the background mix with our heavy breaths.

"That was... better than I had hoped." Scarlett lifts her head. "Arm porn for the win," she says cheekily.

I smack her ass with my hand and her pussy pulses. "Let's get you dressed, and I'll clean up."

"Oh. Okay." I can hear the disappointment in her tone.

"I'm not done with you, Scar. But we both need showers and then I'm taking you in my bed. Nice and slow."

"Or fast and hard against a wall. Either will do," she retorts.

"You had me fast, baby. Now I get to savor you." That's not something I'd say to someone that I'm hooking up with, and we both know it. However, we both pretend otherwise. I stalk off to the chairs and gather our shoes and clothes. Once we're both dressed, and I have the condom in an empty grocery store bag from my earlier stop, I get to work cleaning up our supplies.

Scarlett offers to help, but instead, I carry her to the passenger side of the truck and settle her on the seat. "I've got it. You stay right here." I place a kiss on her plump lips and clean up as if a thunderstorm was looming overhead.

Once in the truck, I reach over, taking her hand in mine. I hold on to her the entire drive to my house. The truck is filled with charged silence. We both know that there is more to come once we get to my place, and we're eager for it.

Pulling into the driveway, I hop out of the truck, and I'm at her door, pulling her into my arms. I toss her over my shoulder, carrying her into the house. Making sure to lock the door, I find my way in the dark to my room, not stopping until I reach the en suite bathroom.

Flipping on the light, I get my first look at her. She has mud on her cheek, her hair is a matted mess of red locks, and her face is flushed. I'm sure I'm fairing the same, if not worse. Reaching into the shower, I turn the water on and slowly start to strip her out of her clothes.

"My turn," she whispers. There's something in her eyes that has me wanting to drop to my knees and promise her the world.

That's impossible. I've known her less than a handful of months, but the desire to do just that burns inside me. Just like earlier, I push those feelings to the back of my mind. Scarlett told me not to let this happen. Hell, I don't know when it happened, just that she's all I think about, and I know that I'm fucked. She's wild and carefree, and she has a plan to travel the world with her camera.

I know how this is going to end, but there's no way in hell I'm going to stop it.

"I'm right behind you," I tell her, nodding toward the shower. She steps forward and places a kiss on my chest, right over my heart, and I swear the fucking organ screams out her name.

I quickly undress, tossing my clothes in a pile on top of hers, making a mental note to throw them in the washer so she has clean clothes to wear home tomorrow. Stepping into the shower, my hands immediately go to her face, and I kiss her.

This kiss is different. It's not hurried or feverish. It's slow and sensual as the warm water cascades over our bodies.

Eventually, I have to pull away. We need to wash off the river water, and then I need her beneath me. Hell, on top of me, beside me... I'll take this woman any way that I can get her.

"Ready to get out?" I ask.

"Yes."

Turning off the water, I step out first, not giving a single fuck that I'm getting the floor soaked as I wrap her in a towel, giving her another for her hair before I take one for myself.

"Do you have a hair dryer?"

"I don't. I'm sorry."

"I'm going to get your sheets all wet."

"Baby, we're going to get them wet regardless."

She blushes, and I kiss her because I want to. Because, how can I not when she's standing in front of me looking like a sex goddess with her flushed cheeks?

"Are you hungry? We never ate."

"No, I'm okay."

"Thirsty? Do you need anything before we go to bed?"

She raises her hand and rests it against my cheek. "Just you, Archer Kincaid. I just need you."

I've heard my brothers talk about feeling as though their heart was melting, but I never understood what it meant. Sure, I had an idea. They're all madly in love with their wives, but I think this is it. I think this is what they meant. The moment when you feel ten feet tall and bulletproof with a beautiful woman telling *you* that you are all that she needs.

Scarlett Hatfield just changed me.

I'm hers.

And while she's here, she's mine.

Willow River
Georgia

HOME OF THE KINCAID BROTHERS · WILLOW RIVER, GA · HOME OF THE KINCAID BROTHERS · WILLOW RIVER, GA · HOME OF THE KINCAID BROTHERS · WILLOW RIVER, GA ·

WWW.KAYLEERYAN.COM

Chapter 14

SCARLETT

IT'S BEEN THREE WEEKS SINCE I've seen Archer, but we talk and text every day. Something changed the night we went fishing. Neither one of us is willing to talk about it, but I'm certain he's felt the shift just as I have.

He's been working long hours. Summer is the busy time of year for him, and he gets laid off in the winter months. When he told me that, my mind immediately went to him visiting me wherever I end up next during that time.

I shut that thought down as soon as it entered my mind. That's not who we are or what we're about. Archer is just one of those rare, really nice guys. He's sexy as hell, and he's genuinely just good. He's easy to want to be around. That's all that this is.

The studio is slow today. We had one shoot on the books this morning in studio, headshots for a relator. That took no time at all, and I found myself working on edits from yesterday's sessions. Palmer is home today with Remi, and that makes me smile. I'm glad that my being here is giving her this extra time with her daughter. I hate that she's going to be back to working more hours when I leave, but we both knew the deal when I signed on. I just didn't expect to develop the friendship that we have. For a girl who spent most of her life as a loner or with her parents, that's a big deal.

My phone vibrates across the desk, and I welcome the interruption pulling me out of my thoughts.

Archer: How's your day going?

Me: The studio is quiet. Just one shoot on the books today. Working on edits. Yours?

Archer: Hot as hell, but I'm getting it in.

Me: Stay hydrated.

Archer: Always.

Me: You working late again tonight?

Archer: More than likely. How about you?

Me: Nope. This is our early day. We close up at three.

Archer: Enjoy your afternoon off.

Me: You know I will.

I'm smiling like a fool. I'm glad Palmer isn't here to witness it. She's been eyeing me suspiciously for the last few weeks. I'm spending more time on my phone than normal, and she hasn't missed that. She gives me that look, the same one my parents would give me growing up when they thought I was hiding something. Palmer has the look perfected.

Shaking out of my thoughts, I pull up my Favorites playlist and get back to editing. I find my groove and get lost in my work. Is it really work if you love it? Realizing I've been sitting for far too long, I stand and stretch just as the chime over the door alerts me that we have a walk-in guest.

"Welcome to Captured Moments. How are you today?" I ask as I turn and freeze.

"Hey, Firecracker."

"Archer. What are you doing here?" He's still in his worn jeans, work T-shirt, and dusty work boots.

"I took the afternoon off. I wasn't sure I'd make it before you left for the day."

I glance up at the wall, and sure enough, it's five minutes before three. I really did lose track of time. "You took the rest of the day off?" I don't know why I ask. I mean, he just told me he did. "Why?" I ask.

"Do you want the real reason or the reason I came up with on the way here?" He smiles sheepishly.

"Both." I return his smile.

"So, the reason I came up with is that I've been working a shit ton of hours and decided a few hours of vacation time was in order, and I'm craving the food trucks that come to the park in Harris."

"And the real reason?"

"Well, they're both kind of real, but the initial reason?" I nod. "I missed you, Scar."

My chest heaves with how those four words hit me in my feels. "We talk every day."

"Not good enough."

"Lines are being blurred," I tell him.

He nods. "I know."

"I'm leaving, Archer. It's not a maybe thing, like Crosby. I am leaving. I'm chasing my dream."

"I want that for you, Scarlett. More than anything, I want you to have everything you've ever wanted, even if that takes you away from me."

"Then what are we doing? This was supposed to be fun." His words and his support of my dreams mean everything to me. It's hitting me hard that I've found a man who doesn't want to change me. He simply wants to stand next to me. I wish things were different. I wish I had the courage to ask him to stay by my side.

"Are you not having fun with me?" he asks.

"You know I am. But this"—I place my hand over my chest— "isn't supposed to be a part of that."

He closes the distance between us. Lifting my hand, he places it over his heart. "It's too late, Scarlett."

"This is going to end with both of us miserable."

He shrugs. "I know that you're a free spirit. I know that you want to travel for your photography. I know that you're only here for a short amount of time. I also know that I can't stay away from you during that time. I don't want to, Scarlett. I'm a grown man. I know the risks. I know that once your contract is up, you're leaving Willow River. I know that, and I still want you."

"We should stop this." My words are whispered as if maybe if I'm the only one that hears them, then they won't be true.

"Probably," he agrees. "I know that you tried to warn me not to fall for you, but I blame you."

"What?" His words cause my heart to twist inside my chest. I'm surprised, yet when I think about Archer and the way I feel when we're together, the way he treats me, I know I shouldn't be.

A grin pulls at his lips. "You're too easy to fall for, Scar. Does this make us crazy that we're setting ourselves up for heartbreak? Yeah, but I still don't care. I'd rather have this time with you, being honest with how I'm falling for you, than not have you at all."

"Really?" My heart races. I've never had someone other than my parents choose me, not like this. I have this warm feeling in my chest.

"Yes. Really." He reaches out and wraps his arms around me, embracing me with his strong arms. I melt into him. I can't remember ever receiving a better hug or feeling as safe and as content as I do at this very moment.

"Are you ready to get out of here?" he asks, still holding on to me. "Is there anything I can help you do to close up?"

"Yeah, I'm ready." I pull back from him. "I just need to pack up my camera and laptop and lock up."

"Let's do that. We can go back to my place. I need a shower, and then you can tell me how you're feeling about this. About us."

"Okay." I'm distracted. My mind is a video reel of our conversation as I step away and go about packing up my camera. I keep it with me at all times. Next is my laptop, and when I turn to face Archer, he holds his hands out for both. I don't argue with him that I can handle them or that I do every day. He's offering because he's that nice of a guy. Not because he thinks I can't do it on my own. He just doesn't want me to when he's there to help me with it.

"Ready?" he asks.

"Yes." I move toward the door, turn off the lights, flip the sign to Closed, and step out the door, making sure that it's locked behind us. Side by side, we walk to my car, which is parked beside the building. I hit the Unlock button on my key fob and pull open the back door. Archer places my things inside and closes the door softly.

Then he's kissing me. It's slow and sweet, just like the man himself.

"I'll see you at home," he says. He reaches around me and opens my door for me. I slide in behind the wheel and pretend that this is normal. That this man hasn't just flipped me and my heart upside down with his surprise visit and subsequent confession.

Twenty minutes later, I'm sitting on Archer's couch, a pillow on my lap to rest my laptop on as I skim over the images I took the night we went fishing. I haven't seen him to show him. I sent him a few screenshots, but I'm excited to show him everything from that night.

Archer is upstairs in the shower while I make myself at home on his couch. It's a new concept for me. I can honestly say the only place I've ever felt I could just relax and be me was at my parents'. I had to sell the house to pay the medical bills, and that's when I started to travel.

I no longer had a home.

Nowhere felt like home.

That's when I decided I would pursue travel photography. I always loved it when we went on family vacations, and it made me feel closer to my parents. Now, here I sit, feeling like I might actually belong on this couch with the man who owns it.

"Sorry, I needed that." Archer sits next to me on the couch, his hair still wet from his shower.

"That's the fastest shower ever." I laugh.

"I didn't want to keep you waiting. Get in, get it done, and get out." He nods at my laptop. "What are we looking at?"

"The images I took the night we went fishing."

"Really?" His eyes light with interest.

"Yeah, I thought you might want to see them."

"Definitely." He turns a little to the side and slides his arm over my shoulders so that I'm cradled into his chest. "Show me the goods."

There's a part of me that wants to toss my laptop to the side and strip for him, but I know that's not what he means. Being near this man does things to me unlike anything I've ever felt before.

Slowly, I start moving through the images that I have pulled up, taking up my entire screen. "Scarlett," Archer breathes. "Babe, these are incredible."

"Thanks. The lighting that night was perfect." I flip to the next image. It's of Archer standing looking out at the river. The sun is setting in the background, and the field of flowers pulls it all together.

"You should sell these."

"What? No, I mean, yeah, that's the plan, but not these."

"Why not these? They're great."

"This night was just for us."

His lips press against my temple. "Our night," he says softly. "Show me more. Where are some other places that you've worked or traveled to?"

I glance over my shoulder at him. "Are you sure you want to see it?"

"I'm sure."

I'm giddy to show him my portfolio. "This is what I used for my interview with Palmer." I flip through the images I've taken in my travels, both alone and with my parents. "It's capturing a memory. A moment in time that will forever live on from the image."

It must be a photographer thing. "Palmer did good naming her business Captured Moments."

"She really did."

We spend the next hour scrolling through images. I even open a folder that contains only my parents. "I miss them," I say softly.

Archer doesn't tell me he understands. He doesn't tell me it will get easier with time. He takes my laptop from me and places it on the coffee table, then lifts me onto his lap and gives me another one of his soul-soothing hugs. Hot tears well behind my eyes. Archer must sense my pending breakdown as he holds me tighter and runs his hand over my hair.

"I've got you, baby."

I don't know if it's the four words, the sentiment, the man, or all three. But I lose the battle of holding off my tears. I let them fall freely in the safety of his arms. He never wavers as he holds me tightly, running his fingers through my hair.

I cry for the loss of my parents, for the loneliness that I feel, and for the man who's making me feel like maybe I'm not so alone. The man who makes my heart beat faster. The one who's holding me as if I'm precious to him, and maybe, just maybe, I think I might be.

I know he's precious to me.

I also know it's going to kill me to walk away from him, but I have to follow my dreams. I can't let something like my heart stop me. I vowed to follow my passion when my parents died, and I plan to do that. I also plan to spend as much time with Archer as I can while I'm here. He's right. I'd rather have this time with him and a sad heart when I have to leave than never experience moments like this.

Missing out on knowing Archer Kincaid would be one of life's greatest tragedies.

I sit up, wiping at my tear-stained cheeks. "I want this time with you," I blurt. "You said we could talk about it. We don't really need to."

"Yeah?" he asks, hope in his eyes.

I nod. "It's going to hurt like hell to walk away from you, Archer Kincaid."

"We have months before that happens. Right now, I just want to enjoy the time that we have."

"In another life..." My voice trails off.

"Are you hungry?" he asks, and I'm grateful for the change in subject. It's out there, and now I don't want to talk about it or think about the end of my time here in Willow River.

"Yes. I worked through lunch."

"Scarlett," he scolds.

"I was working."

"You have to eat." He brushes my hair back out of my eyes.

"Then feed me, Kincaid."

"What sounds good?"

"Can you cook?"

"I do all right. I'm not going to be running my own restaurant anytime soon." He chuckles.

"What would you be making if I weren't here?"

"I'd planned to make buffalo chicken pasta, but I was going to cheat and use canned chicken because it's so much faster and tastes the same. Do you like spicy food?"

"How spicy are we talking? Like ghost pepper spicy or buffalo wing spicy?"

"Wing spicy."

"Yep. Can I help?"

"No. But you can keep me company." With a quick kiss, he stands from the couch with me in his arms.

"I feel like I should tell you that I can walk, but it's sexy how you carry me around. It makes me feel... some kind of way." I almost told him it made me feel wanted. It's bad enough I'm falling for him, and I've admitted that. I don't need to add fuel to the heartbreak fire.

"Is this 'some kind of way' a good thing?" he asks, raising his brows.

"Yeah, Popeye, it's a good thing."

"Good." He pops a kiss on my nose and settles me onto the kitchen island.

"So how do we make this culinary excellence?" I ask.

"Two cans of chicken, drained, buffalo sauce, cream cheese, ranch dressing, and pasta."

"That's it?"

"Yep. It's basically buffalo chicken dip, which is one of my favorites. I just added pasta because I needed more sustenance than chips and dip." He laughs.

"So you thought this up on your own?"

"Yes, ma'am," he says proudly.

"I'm excited to try it. I love buffalo chicken dip." My mouth waters just thinking about it.

"Something we have in common." He gives me a smile that is boyish and sexy at the same time. Heat rushes between my thighs. At the same time, my heart races for how quickly I've become attached to him.

"That thing is lethal." I point to his smile, which only makes him smile wider.

He leans in, puckering his lips for a kiss. He looks ridiculous, but I indulge him anyway.

"Are you sure I can't help?" I say after a quick peck.

"Nah, I've got this. Tell me something about you that I don't already know."

"Hmm...." I tap my index finger against my chin. "Oh, Butter Pecan Ice Cream is life," I moan at the thought of a big ole bowl right now.

"Damn, that's a deal breaker."

"What?" I ask, my mouth dropping open.

"Nah, I'm just messing with you. It's going to take more than that to pull me away from you."

"Mean."

"What else?"

"I used to hate my red hair when I was little. I was made fun of all the time at school, and I begged my parents to let me dye it. My mom always smiled and said one day, I would grow into it. She was right. I love it now."

"It's beautiful."

"Flattery will get you everywhere, Kincaid."

"Not flattery. It's honesty."

"You're refreshing."

"How so?"

"I don't ever have to guess what this is between us. You're not afraid to talk about the hard stuff. You're open and honest, and that's rare these days. I'm used to men who want to play head games or sleep with me and move on."

His eyes darken. "Idiots," he mutters.

"There haven't been many. In fact, I was nineteen when I lost my virginity."

"Really?"

"Yeah. I'd just lost my mom. There was a guy I worked with at a local coffee shop while taking photography classes. I was hurting, and one thing led to another. It wasn't memorable, and I hated that I made the decision when I was hurting."

"What happened to the guy?"

"Turns out he was moving. He'd given his notice that day, and I didn't know it. He dropped me off at my place, and I never saw him again. I cried myself to sleep that night, but it wasn't just about him. I missed my mom."

"He didn't deserve that gift."

"You're right, but I was alone and grieving and seeking any kind of contact I could get." I pause before blurting out what's on my mind. "I wish it had been you."

He stills. "Scarlett." There is so much in the simple muttering of my name. Longing, pain, pity, and so much more that I can't even name.

I shrug. "Live and learn, but I can't help but think how you would have made sure I was okay."

He drops the spoon he was mixing the chicken with. He dries his hands on a hand towel and cradles my cheeks with his large hands. "Always, Scarlett. I know you're leaving. I know you're chasing your dreams, and that's what I want for you, but I want you to listen to me, baby. Can you do that?" I nod. "I don't care how much time has passed. I don't care where you are in the world. If you ever need me, you've got me."

"That's a big promise, Popeye."

"And you know that I don't break my promises." He kisses me tenderly. His lips are soft as they press against mine. It's a chaste kiss compared to others we've shared, but no less intense. It makes me question everything I thought about my future. Could this man be a part of it?

WILLOW RIVER

HOME OF THE KINCAID BROTHERS · WILLOW RIVER, GA · HOME OF THE KINCAID BROTHERS · WILLOW RIVER, GA · HOME OF THE KINCAID BROTHERS · WILLOW RIVER, GA · HOME OF THE KINCAID BROTHERS · WILLOW RIVER, GA ·

Willow River
Georgia

WWW.KAYLEERYAN.COM

Chapter 15

ARCHER

I THOUGHT THE DAY RAMSEY married Deacon was the happiest I'd ever seen her. That was true up until today. My little cousin, only in size, not in age, as we're the same age, is glowing. She hasn't stopped smiling all day, and Deacon, her husband, his smile rivals hers.

I'm happy for them.

I'm not sure when baby showers started being co-ed. Apparently, it's the in thing now. That's what Scarlett tells me. I don't know much about baby showers. My brothers keep having babies, and when I'm invited, I attend. Of course, I do. They're my brothers, and that baby is my niece or nephew, or in this case, little cousin, but it's the same situation. Ramsey is like a sister to me.

"Baby girl, maybe one day soon you'll be a big sister," Brooks coos to his daughter, Remi.

"She just turned one," I remind him. "Maybe let her get out of diapers first."

"I want my kids close together like we were."

"And is Palmer okay with this plan?"

"Yeah." He smiles.

I'm ready to tell him I'm happy for them when laughter rings out. I turn to follow the familiar sound, and sure enough, it's Scarlett. She's sitting on the couch, with Blakely on her lap, letting Blake take a few pictures of Ramsey as she helps her hold the camera. Her long auburn hair is hanging down her back in soft curls. My hands fist at my sides. I can practically feel the silky strands beneath my fingertips.

"Speaking of babies. That smolder could get her pregnant from here."

I have to force myself to tear my gaze from Scarlett to listen to whatever it is Brooks is going on about. "What?"

He laughs. Remi grins and laughs, too, because her daddy is. Reaching over, I take her from his arms, and she snuggles into my chest. Damn, I love being an uncle.

"That intense stare you're giving Scarlett, Arch, it's written all over your face how bad you want her."

"She's already mine," I tell him. I sound smug, and I don't give a fuck.

"I heard that." He nods. "She still leaving?"

Brooks knows the exact details of Scarlett's employment contract with Palmer. I'm sure his wife filled him in. Hell, I'm sure my entire family knows. Brooks is the first to bring it up, and I feel a big brother, be careful speech coming on.

Nothing I haven't already told myself in the last few months since Scarlett appeared in my life.

"Yeah, she's still leaving. She's crazy fu—freaking talented," I correct, smiling at my niece in my arms.

"You're setting yourself up for pain. Damn, Archer, did you not learn anything from watching Ryder?" he asks.

"That's different. Jordyn left without saying goodbye. I know Scarlett is leaving. She's chasing her dreams."

"So is Jordyn."

"It's different."

"What? Do you think it's going to work out for you like it did for Rush? That she's going to change her mind and stay here?"

"That was different too. Crosby wanted to stay. She just wasn't sure she was going to be able to. I'm fine, Brooks," I assure him. "I know what I'm doing."

"Signing up to have your heart torn in two?"

"I'd rather have this time with her than not have her at all."

"Fuck," he mutters under his breath. I'm not sure if the low mutter is just him in disbelief at my words or because he doesn't want his daughter to hear. Either way, the meaning is the same. He knows my mind is made up, and nothing he can do or say will change it. It's a Kincaid trait. Once we know, we know.

"What happens when she's gone, Arch? Are you going to live the rest of your life alone? What about a wife and kids?" He nods to where I'm snuggling Remi.

"I don't know," I confess. "I didn't say I was in love with her. I said I'd rather have the time than miss out on her."

"Open your eyes, Archer. It's written all over your face."

"Remi, tell Daddy that he's seeing things." I tickle her side, and she wiggles in my arms. Her cute little laugh reaching in and grabbing hold of my heart.

"Baby hog," Ryder says, joining us. He opens his arms for Remi, and she leans out for him to take her.

"We need more babies. There are not enough for all of us," I grump.

"I'm trying." Brooks chuckles. Our earlier conversation is now tabled for another time. I know he won't mention it in front of Ryder. The poor guy has been nursing his broken heart for far too long. He doesn't need Brooks to remind him of the pain of Jordyn leaving without saying goodbye.

"Well, hurry, would you?" Ryder fires back.

"You want to watch her for a few hours later?" Brooks wags his eyebrows.

"You want to come home with Uncle Ry?" he asks Remi. She just grins and lays her head on his chest. "Damn, how do you leave her at all?" he asks.

"It's tough," Brooks admits. "I used to think that Declan was just overprotective of Blakely. Always calling to check on her and reminding us not to curse. I get it now. She's a piece of me and

Palmer, and damn if that's not the strongest kind of love I've ever felt in my life."

"Do you mind?" Scarlett steps in front of us and holds up her camera.

Remi lifts her head and smiles big. I'm sure she's used to her photographer momma pointing the camera at her. Scarlett smiles at my brothers before turning her gaze to me. There is so much in that look. Longing, desire, need, and something softer. She waves and walks away, and my eyes follow her across the room, where she snaps a picture of Maverick and Merrick with bows in their hair.

"You're in trouble, brother. So much trouble," Ryder tells me.

I hate that my brothers are right, but there isn't much I can do about it at this point.

I won't walk away from this.

From her.

I can't.

"Today was a good day," Scarlett says from the passenger seat of my truck. She rode with me to Deacon and Ramsey's, and now we're heading back to my place.

"It was. I'm happy for them. Ramsey didn't always have an easy life. She deserves the happiness that Deacon brings her."

"Aw, Archer Kincaid, are you a secret romantic?" she teases.

"Nah, just honest."

"You are that," she agrees.

"So, what do you want to do the rest of the night?"

"Honestly? Nothing. Can we just do nothing?"

"Yes, but only because you said we."

She chuckles as she kicks off her sandals and curls her feet under her in the seat. I glance over to make sure her seat belt is still buckled. I ease off the gas just a little and keep my eyes on the road.

"Should we pick up some food?"

"Depends. Do you have food at your place?"

"I have leftovers from last night's dinner."

"That cheesy chicken and rice stuff you were talking about?"

"Yeah."

"That works for me. Wait, do we still have ice cream in the freezer?"

We. "I added more to my grocery order that I picked up Wednesday night."

"The drumsticks?"

"Your favorite." I nod, keeping my eyes on the road when all I really want to do is keep them on her.

"You spoil me, Popeye." Her tone is light and teasing, and I love it.

I've never been this relaxed with a woman before. Hell, I've never had this much fun with a woman before. Even if we're just sitting around my house watching movies or talking, it's more fun than any night out from my past.

I'm aware that if my brothers could hear my thoughts, they'd be razzing me. My mind drifts to my earlier conversation with Brooks. I know I'm going to be torn up when she rides out of town, leaving me in my hometown. I've run this over and over in my mind. I need to work. I can't work while traveling. That's not who I am. I'm a brick mason. I have a job that I go to every day. Sure, we travel from jobsite to jobsite, but that's different. I can't just float from city to city or hell, country to country, hoping to find mason work while we're there. The life of a free spirit isn't for me, but that doesn't mean I can't care for one.

Care. I more than care about her. But just like the thought of her leaving, I'm pushing those feelings deep down somewhere I can pretend to overlook them. I'm not naive enough to think that it's going to hurt less by ignoring what she means to me, but that's my plan right now, and I'm sticking to it.

"You should plant some flowers," she muses as we pull into the driveway.

"I don't have time to worry about keeping them alive."

"Maybe even a hanging basket."

"You do know I'm a man living alone, right?"

"What's that supposed to mean?"

"Just how it sounds. Men don't care about flowers and all that."

"Some men do."

I nod. "Okay, you're right, but this man doesn't."

"It would really brighten the place up," she comments.

Turning off the truck, I turn to look at her. "Do you want to plant flowers or get a hanging basket?" I ask her.

"Oh, there is no point planting for my place , I'll be gone, but I do have a basket."

"And what is required to keep whatever is growing in this basket alive?" I ask her.

"You just have to water it every day. You know, show it a little love."

"And if I kill it? Are you going to be upset with me?"

"Not at all."

I nod. "All right, let's go see if we can find a hanging basket."

"Really?" Her eyes light up.

"Unless you want to wait and go tomorrow?"

She thinks it over for a few seconds. "Tomorrow is better. I really just want to—" She pauses.

"You really just want to what, Scar?" It doesn't matter what she says. I'm in.

"I just want you to lay with me. Just be with you tonight." Her voice is small, and my heart gallops in my chest.

"Done." I reach for my handle and climb out of my truck. I'm almost to her door when it opens. "You're supposed to wait on me," I remind her.

She sticks out her tongue. "I get it. You're a true gentleman, but I can open my own door. Besides, maybe I wanted to open your door for you." She jumps out of the cab of my truck, landing expertly on her feet, and places her hands on her hips, staring up at me.

"I open the door for you, baby. That's how this works."

"Well, we don't always have to play by your rules, Archer Kincaid."

"How's this for following your rules?" I bend and lift her over my shoulder, slamming her door shut and stalking toward the front door.

Her hands swat at my ass. "Since when is this my rule?" She giggles.

"Since you told me you thought it was sexy."

"This is sexy." She smacks my ass again.

I shake my head, and I manage to enter the code, opening my front door. Kicking off my shoes, I carry her to the couch, dropping her easily. Her laughter has my face splitting into a grin. "I stand behind my words. So sexy."

Bracing my hands on either side of her, I lean in for a kiss. "You're sexy." I kiss her again before standing tall. "I'm going to heat us up some dinner. Pull us up something to watch."

"Okay. What are you in the mood for?" she calls after me.

"Anything." I get to work heating up two bowls of chicken and rice and pop two pieces of garlic bread into the toaster. "What do you want to drink?" I call out to her.

"What are my choices?"

I bury my head in the fridge and announce her options, "Beer, water, tea, and root beer."

"Am I staying here?"

I lift my head to look at her, where she's kneeling on my couch. Her hair is now pulled up in a messy knot on her head, the remote is in her hand, and her head is tilted to the side as she waits for my answer.

"Yes."

She nods. "Beer, please."

I don't tell her that she could just live here and save her money for wherever it is she travels to when she leaves here, but then we'd have to talk about her leaving, and I don't like to think about it, let alone talk about it. Besides, if she lived here— I rub my hand over my chest to alleviate the ache that's forming just thinking about how much closer we would grow.

Yeah, as much as I'd love to offer, I keep my mouth shut. I don't think that either one of us could handle her leaving if we were to take that step. Sleepovers, however, are a necessity.

I take our beers into the living room, placing them on the table. I steal a kiss, because there will be a day when I'll miss being able to taste her lips anytime that I want. "Here you go," I say, handing her a steaming bowl of chicken and cheesy rice and a perfectly crisped piece of garlic toast.

"Thank you."

I sit next to her on the couch, so close that our thighs are touching, but she doesn't seem to mind. I watch her closely as she takes a bite. When she smiles, I relax. I don't know what the hell I was worried about. I know it's good. I made it, but if she didn't like it, I was heading right back to the kitchen to make her something else.

"This is so good." She takes another big bite, and I dig into mine as well.

It doesn't take us long to polish off our dinner. "Ready for your ice cream?" I ask, and I take her empty bowl, placing it on top of mine.

"Not right now. I'll help with those." She starts to stand, but I raise my hand, stopping her.

"I'm just going to put them in the dishwasher and start it. My breakfast dishes are in there. Give me five minutes, and we can start the movie. Do you need anything else? Another beer?"

"Water?"

"You got it." I make quick work of loading the dishwasher and grabbing us both a bottle of water. I turn off the lights, leaving the one over the stove on, and take my seat next to her on the couch.

"You know I'm a sure thing, right?" Her lips are tilted up into a warm smile. "You trying to set the mood?"

"No. That's not what I was trying to do. I'll fuck you in broad daylight, Firecracker."

An adorable pink coats her cheeks. "Right." She clears her throat.

"You want to test that theory?" I nod toward the sliding glass door in the kitchen that leads out to the back deck. "We still have some daylight left."

"In your backyard?" she gasps.

I shrug like I couldn't care less who sees, and part of that is true. They can see me, but not her. Never her. "Or we could just stick to the plan and watch the movie. It's up to you."

"Movie," she croaks.

I toss my head back in laughter and slide my arm around her shoulders, pulling her into me. "You change your mind, baby. You let me know."

"No. That's— Nope. I'm good. I'm a free spirit, not an exhibitionist."

Leaning into her, I place my lips next to her ear. "Can I tell you a secret?" She nods. "I'd never let anyone see you like that." Her body instantly relaxes. "Never, Scarlett."

"There he is," she says. She turns and places her lips just beneath my chin. "I thought you'd been abducted by aliens."

"What?" I chuckle. I never know what's going to come out of her mouth.

"You weren't being my sweet Archer. I mean, your mouth is dirty when we're... getting dirty, but this was something different. I thought you were into that."

"No. I'm not into sharing or showing. Ever."

"That's a relief." She snuggles in closer and pushes Play. I don't even bother to look at the screen. Instead, I close my eyes and enjoy the fact that she's here in my arms, and that's all that matters right now. Sharing this night with her. Laughing and just being together.

Chapter 16

SCARLETT

I DON'T KNOW HOW IT'S already September. Usually, time drags by, but it seems as though my time here in Willow River is fading fast. The excitement of what's to come isn't as strong as it usually is, either, but I know why or who is responsible for that.

Speaking of Archer, he's going to be here any minute. I need to get moving. I pull the black short-sleeve cotton top over the top of the red corset. The black shirt is low cut and allows the lace of my red corset to show through. It's a little sexy for a Labor Day cookout at his brother's, but I want to look good for him, and I blame Palmer. We were shopping online at the studio a couple of weeks ago, and she encouraged me to get one. I told her I would if she would. I ended up with the red and Palmer with the deep blue.

I made my mom's chicken ranch pasta salad for today. I'm grabbing the container out of the fridge when Archer knocks on the door. "Come in," I call out to him.

"Just me," he says.

"I know." I smile at him. He moves to me, wrapping his arms around my waist, kissing me soundly. "Hi," I say when he pulls back.

"You shouldn't tell just anyone to come in, Scar."

"I knew you were due any minute." He scowls at my reply, but I hand him the container of pasta before he can give me more of a hard time. "I need to grab my camera, and I'm ready." I kiss his jaw and rush to the other side of the small kitchen where my camera bag sits. I take my battery off the charger and zip up the bag, tossing it over my shoulder. "Ready?"

"Let me take that." Archer reaches out for my camera bag.

"I've got it, Popeye. Give those guns a rest, yeah?" I tease. He shakes his head, but a smile plays on his lips.

"Where's your bag?"

"What bag?"

"You're staying with me tonight, right?"

I debate about messing with him, telling him I don't want to stay with him tonight, but that would be a lie, and there is so much hope in his voice I can't do it. "It's by the door."

"Good." He nods and moves toward the door, grabbing my overnight bag. "Is there anything in here that can't be in the truck while we're at Sterling's?" he asks.

"Nope. It should be fine."

"Are you sure? We can take it back to my place first."

"Positive. Thank you for checking. Sweet Archer is out to play today."

"Well, after seeing that peek of red poking out from beneath your shirt, that might change later." He wags his eyebrows, and I crack up laughing as I follow him to his truck.

I'm holding my stomach with one hand and my camera in the other. Bending at the waist, I try to catch my breath. I'm laughing too hard. I close my eyes to try and block it out, but I can still hear the song, and the image of Maverick and Merrick dancing to the post of the patio, pretending it's a stripper pole, has me unable to catch my breath.

"S-Stop," I stutter. "You have to stop." I feel an arm wrap around my waist, and I know without looking that it's Archer. He's been more touchy-feely with me today in front of his family. More so than he ever has, and it's been nice—to feel like I'm a part of something. This family, my relationship with Archer. All of it. This day has been one of the best.

"Get your dollars out!" Maverick swivels his hips as he drops to the floor, shaking his ass.

"Porn Star Dancing" by My Darkest Days plays over the outdoor speakers. "Thankfully, the kids are all down for naps, and Blakely went home with my parents. They would be scarred for life after this debacle." Archer laughs. The husky sound causes chills to race down my spine.

Will I ever not respond to him like it's the first time he's touching me? I hope not.

"Right?" I lean into his hold, a smile on my face as I watch his two youngest brothers entertain us. When the song finally ends, we all clap and cheer for them.

"Now," Merrick speaks up. "If the ladies think they can rival that...." He waves his arm as if to say they should take the stage.

"Scarlett." Palmer stands and pulls off the black short-sleeve cardigan she's wearing. Underneath is her blue corset, just like mine. She, too, is wearing a pair of cutoff jean shorts. "Let's do this."

"What? No. Nope."

"Come on. We dance around the studio all the time."

"That's different."

"We match." Palmer points to her corset. "Please?" She sticks out her bottom lip.

"Show us what you've got, Firecracker," Archer urges. He's had a few beers, and I can smell them on his breath. He checked with me beforehand, and I agreed to drive us home in his monster of a truck, and Sterling and Alyssa offered for us to stay here with them, but I'm fine not drinking. It's nice to let Archer let loose with his family. He's usually the one making sure he's taking care of me. He's been working long hours all summer. He deserves this night to chill with his family.

"Fine." I turn and point a finger at Archer. "You cannot get pissed off."

He furrows his brow. "Why would I get pissed off?"

Instead of answering him, I step forward, which causes his arms to fall where they were wrapped around me. Lifting my camera over my head, I hand it to Crosby. She's due any day, and I know that no roughhousing will happen next to her. "Keep this safe for me," I tell her.

"Can I take pictures?" She grins, and I nod.

I take a minute to show her how to operate the basic function and then face Archer. "I mean it. No getting pissed off."

"It's just dancing, Firecracker." His eyes are glassy, but his speech isn't slurred. He's still sober enough to remember this. He's shirtless with his hair slicked back, and his muscled chest with his arms should be illegal. Seriously, I get to go home with this man.

"I'm glad you said that." Gripping the hem of my shirt, I lift it over my head. "Hold on to this for me," I tell him, tossing the shirt at his face.

"Scarlett." I turn to look at him and wink. He reaches out for me, and I let him pull me into his chest. "You're beautiful." He presses a sweet kiss against my lips.

"Come on, lover boy, let her go," someone calls out. I don't bother to turn and look.

"Come back to me."

I melt at his words. "We'll see," I say, teasing him. Turning on my heel, I move to stand next to Palmer, who's already positioned at the post of the porch. "How are we doing this?"

"I don't know how you're doing it, but I'm trying to rile my husband up." I look over her shoulder at Brooks, whose heated stare is on his wife.

"Mission accomplished," I tell her with a laugh.

"What about you?"

I shrug. "Just having a good time. It will be a good laugh."

"Something tells me there won't be as much laughter as there was with the twins. Those two are a riot."

"What are you waiting for, ladies?" Maverick calls out. "Are you afraid you can't compete?" he taunts us.

"Music," Palmer tells him.

The familiar beat of the same song the twins were dancing to flows through the speakers, and Palmer and I share a grin. She grabs one side of the pole, and I grab the other, and we begin to move. I pretend that there is no one but Archer watching me, and I'm sure Palmer is doing the same.

I shake my hips and drop low, letting my ass hit the concrete before bouncing back up and grinding against the pole. Palmer steps around the pole and places her hands on my hips, and we rock to the beat of the song.

"Cut!" Brooks calls out. He's out of his chair and striding toward us. He doesn't look pissed off. No, that's not anger in his eyes. It's lust. And those eyes are only for his wife. He reaches Palmer and lifts her over his shoulder, much like Archer does to me. "Bro, Alyssa, thanks for having us. We're collecting our kid and leaving."

"Let her stay," Sterling tells him. "You can pick her up later, or she can spend the night."

"Go. We've got her," Alyssa adds.

"You"—Brooks points at his brother—"are tonight's favorite." He grins, smacks Palmer on the ass as she lifts her head and waves, and they disappear around the side of the house.

"At least he didn't go inside and wake up all the kids with his caveman act." Orrin laughs.

I feel a hand on my shoulder and his heat against my back. I turn my head as he leans in close. "Looks like you lost your dance partner."

I can feel his bare chest against the parts of my back that are exposed, and even through his jeans and mine, I can feel he's hard for me. "Archer."

"Yeah, Firecracker?" he asks, kissing down my neck.

"It's time for us to go home."

His hands land on my hips, and he squeezes gently. "It will just be us at home."

My heart thuds against my chest, just as it always does when it sounds as if he's referring to his house as our home. "I'm not much into having an audience."

"But you'll have me?" He slides his hand around my waist and pushes the evidence of his hard cock into my ass.

"Yeah, Popeye. I'll have you."

"We're heading out," Archer calls out to his family.

"You need some pointers before you go?" Maverick teases.

"Fuck off," Archer says with zero heat in his tone.

I turn to look at Alyssa and Sterling. "Thank you for having us."

"Thank you for coming. Oh, your container." Alyssa starts to stand, but I wave her off. "I'll get it some other time." I then turn toward Crosby. "Good luck, Momma. Let us know if there is anything we can do when the little one gets here."

"Tonight," Rushton announces, "the baby is supposed to be here tonight."

"These things take time," Crosby says, resting her hands on her baby bump.

"We've waited forever. I want to know what we're having and meet them. The next one we're finding out. I can't handle this waiting business."

"There are very few true surprises in life, Rush." Crosby laughs.

"The surprise is that you love me enough to have a baby with me. The rest is just us." He kisses her sweetly, and I feel a warmness in my chest, watching the love that they share.

"Let us know," I tell them.

We continue making our rounds saying goodbye, and I gather my camera bag before I lead us out to Archer's truck. Once he's in, I shut the door and climb into the driver's side. I start the truck, then adjust the mirrors and the seat to suit me.

"Damn," Archer mutters.

I look over to find him staring at me. "What?"

"I didn't know seeing you drive my truck would turn me on this much." He grips his hard length through his jeans.

"I don't think it's me driving the truck."

"It's you, baby. Trust me on that. You going to ride me when we get home?" he asks.

"Is that what you want?" I ignore the heat that pools between my thighs and inwardly curse at another pair of ruined panties courtesy of this man.

"Hell, yes, that's what I want."

"Okay. Well, I better get us to your place."

"Home, Scar. Take us home." He reaches over and rests his hand on my thigh.

My hands grip the wheel so tightly my knuckles are white. It has nothing to do with driving this beast of a truck and everything to do with the man who owns it. There have been so many moments in the past few months that I've shared with him that make my heart ache. This man, and his kind, sexy demeanor has found a permanent spot for himself inside my hardened heart. I don't know how he did it, but he lives there rent-free.

I didn't expect Archer Kincaid, but I will forever be a better person for knowing this incredible man.

Once we're in the house, Archer plops down on the couch and pats his lap. "Come sit with me."

"Why don't we get you in bed?" I suggest. If he passes out down here, no way can I get him to the bedroom. He doesn't seem the type to pass out drunk, but once you sit and stop moving, it can sneak up on you.

"Because I want to snuggle." There is no further mention of what he asked about in the truck, so I keep my mouth shut and take a seat on his lap. He wraps his strong arms around me, and I sink into his embrace.

"I like this," he says, playing with the straps of my corset.

"I thought you might. I almost didn't buy it. Palmer talked me into it."

"Remind me to thank her."

"I'm pretty sure Brooks is taking care of that for you."

He chuckles. "Are you hungry or thirsty?"

"No. I'm good." The silence stretches between us. He doesn't stop touching me. His fingers feel feather light as they trace across my skin.

"You ready for bed?" he asks several minutes later, as his hand leisurely strokes up and down my back.

"I am if you are." I don't move. I'm too comfortable.

"With you, baby, I'm always ready." He taps my thigh, and I stand, offering him my hand. He takes it and automatically entwines his fingers with mine. Hand in hand, we turn out the lights and make our way down the hall to his bedroom. Archer leads us to his side of the bed and switches on the lamp.

"You ready to ride me, beautiful Scarlett?" he asks, cradling my face in the palm of his hand.

"Are you still"—I glance down at his crotch—"up for it?"

He scoffs. "I stay hard when you're around. Fuck, even if I hear your name."

"Then I'd say you better start stripping."

"Fuck me, and it's hot when you take charge."

Offering him a flirty grin, I get to work on stripping out of my own clothes. He stands still, his eyes burning as he watches me. "You're behind, Kincaid," I tell him as I drop the corset to the floor.

His reflexes are slower as he reaches both arms out to cup a breast in each hand. He tests their weight before stepping closer, dipping his head and sucking a hard nipple into his mouth. I bury my hands in his hair, enjoying his mouth on me. He moves to the other breast as his hand slides down to my jean shorts. He pops the button and slides his hand inside my panties.

"Is all this for me?" he asks as he explores my pussy with his fingers.

"Archer."

"Yeah, baby?"

"You're supposed to be getting naked."

"I will," he says, still teasing me with his fingers.

"Please."

He pulls his fingers from my panties and brings them to his mouth. I don't know why but watching him place them into his mouth and suck turns me on more than anything ever has. Maybe it has something to do with the groan that emits from his throat or how his eyes roll before closing as if he's tasting the most decadent of desserts.

He steps back and pulls his shirt over his head. This time it's my turn to stand and watch as he exposes his body to me.

"Like what you see?" He smirks.

"You know I do."

"Lose the shorts and panties, Firecracker." He's naked as the day he was born when he climbs onto the bed and lies back against the fluffy pillows.

Breaking out of my trance, I do as he says, stripping out of the remainder of my clothes. I have one knee on the bed, ready to straddle him when he pats his chest. "Come up here."

"What?"

"You heard me. Straddle me here." He taps his chest again.

I don't know where this is going, but I do know there hasn't been a single moment of naked time with this man that I didn't thoroughly enjoy, so I do as I'm asked and straddle him, resting over his chest.

"Up on your knees."

I rise up, and he moves down. He smirks up at me. "Move up a little," he instructs. A shudder rolls through me because now I know where this is going. When he said I was going to ride him, I expected to be riding his cock, not his face.

"Are you sure?" I ask.

"Fucking positive." The words are barely past his lips when he's gripping my thighs and pulling me down on his mouth.

"Oh," I moan. My body lurches forward at the momentum of his tongue massaging my clit. My hands grapple for the headboard to hold myself steady.

His grip on my thighs is tight, but I still manage to lift up on my knees when the sensation is too much.

"Get back here." He smacks my ass, and I yelp in surprise. It doesn't hurt, but I wasn't expecting that.

"I can't," I pant. I need him inside me.

"You can. Give me everything you've got, Firecracker."

I let my earlier thoughts out, "It's too much. I need you inside me."

"Not until you come all over my face." His hands travel to my hips, and he pulls me down onto him. "Good girl," he mutters before he unleashes on me. He eats at me like a starving man, and all I can do is hold on to the headboard and feel.

That deep tingling feeling starts deep in my core, and heat rushes through me like a four-alarm fire. I rock my hips, seeking the release, and Archer grunts his approval. That sound sends me over the edge. I dig my nails into the wood of the bed frame as I still over him, letting the euphoria his tongue has caused roll through my body.

When I finally slacken against him, he somehow manages to lift me, moving me to my back. I force my eyes open to stare up at him. He's got his hard cock in his hand as he licks his lips, which are still shining with my release. He leans over to the nightstand, grabs a condom, has himself sheathed, and is pushing inside me in a matter of seconds. We both moan at the contact.

I expect him to unleash on me, but he does the exact opposite. Archer takes his time. Each stroke is slow, and his hands roam all over my body. My arms are under his, gripping his back as he makes love to me.

We don't make love.

But there is no other way to describe this moment.

The one where Archer Kincaid steals my entire heart.

Willow River
Georgia

HOME OF THE KINCAID BROTHERS · WILLOW RIVER, GA · HOME OF THE KINCAID BROTHERS · WILLOW RIVER, GA · HOME OF THE KINCAID BROTHERS · WILLOW RIVER, GA · HOME OF THE KINCAID BROTHERS

WWW.KAYLEERYAN.COM

Chapter 17

ARCHER

THE DAYS, WEEKS, AND MONTHS are rolling past me at lightning speed. Normally, I don't think too much about the passing of time. However, that's changed since Scarlett appeared in my life. My wild Firecracker. For the first time in my life, I wish that I could slow the hours that pass us by.

It's as if I blinked, and it's already the last week of October. I have five more months with her, and that's not enough time. There will never be enough time where Scarlett is concerned.

I thought I had a handle on my feelings. I enjoyed spending time with her. I never get tired of being around her. In fact, I want to be around her more. I've come close to asking her to move in with me. At first, I was convinced it was a terrible idea, that I'd grow too attached.

It's too late.

I'm already too attached.

It's still probably a terrible idea, but there is no way I'm walking away from the time I have left with her. I'm in this. *We're* in this, and we both plan to see it through until the end.

Her contract is up in five months, and then she's on to her next big adventure. I want that for her, but I want her to stay here with me even more. My heart is torn in two directions, and I struggle with that every damn day. No matter how badly I want her to stay here and start a life with me, I know she's destined for great things. She just doesn't know that she's going to be carrying my heart with her on her journey.

My heart screams at me to beg her to stay, but I won't do that. I can't. I knew the score when I got involved with her, and I know my Scarlett; she's going to be hurting when she leaves, and me begging her to stay would just make it tougher on her. I won't do that to her. No matter how hard I have to bite my tongue and fight the urge to drop to my knees and offer her the world, my world, and my heart and soul to stay.

Fuck, I'm going to miss her.

I pull into her driveway for our date tonight, just the two of us. I love my brothers and sisters-in-law, but I just needed some time with her. She loves haunted houses, and there are a few in our area, and that's what we're doing tonight. We're going to hit as many of them as we can. Before I can get out of the truck and knock on her door, she comes barreling down the front steps. She's wearing black leggings that make her ass look incredible. Whoever invented those damn things, I thank them. She's got on a long sweater and boots that come up just underneath her knees. Her hair hangs in loose curls down her back, and her smile lights up her face. She pulls open the door and climbs inside my truck.

"This is a date," I say once her door is shut.

"I know." She reaches for her seat belt and straps herself in.

I point to the bouquet of flowers I picked up for her sitting on the corner console. "I was coming to your door to get you and give you these." I hand her the flowers.

"Aw, Popeye, no one has ever bought me flowers before." She brings them to her nose to smell them, then turns and carefully lays them on the back floorboard of the truck. "It's cold enough outside. They should be fine there for the night."

"How am I supposed to be romantic when you steal my thunder?" I ask.

"Archer! It's the last week of October. I've been waiting all month for this night. We don't have time for romance. We've got things to do."

I chuckle at her exuberance for the season. "Fine, but next time stay put until I can knock like a real man."

"You're all man, handsome. Trust me on that one."

This. Fucking. Woman.

I lean over the console and slide my hand behind her neck, pulling her into a kiss. She may be in a hurry, but I need a taste before we go. "Missed you," I say, giving her another soft peck before settling back in my seat.

"You saw me last night."

"But you went home."

"Because I don't live with you."

"You should. Then I'd see you more."

"Archer—" she starts, but I shake my head, stopping her.

"I'm allowed to miss my girl."

"I missed you too," she confesses.

I let it go. "You ready?"

"I was born ready. I love Halloween."

"Are you hungry?"

"Um, we're going to have to hit a drive-thru, Kincaid. We cannot waste precious time at a restaurant. The lines will be long because this is the last weekend."

"Fair enough." I laugh. "Our first stop is Harris. Be thinking about what you want to eat, and we'll hit the drive-thru."

"Perfect." She settles back in her seat. "Oh, how's Crosby and baby Caden?" she asks.

"They're both good. Rush is already driving her crazy with his overprotectiveness."

"I wouldn't expect anything less from him or any of your brothers, actually."

"Even me?"

"Um, yes, even you. You're all bossy and commanding. I can only imagine how you will be when your future wife has a baby." There is something in her voice, something that tells me that she's not as blasé about this as she would like for me to think.

I want to tell her that she could be that woman, my wife, the mother of my babies, but I've already made things uncomfortable with us once tonight. "I'd be chill."

"Not a chance."

"Okay, maybe not, but the love of your life and a tiny human that's a part of both of you... that's a big fucking deal, Scar." I realize my words could seem insensitive to her. "I'm sorry, I didn't think," I'm quick to apologize.

She waves me off. "You're right. It is a big deal. You and your brothers, you're all good men." She turns to stare out the window. "Sometimes I like to pretend they were just young and couldn't afford a baby or didn't have family support, and they wanted to give me a better life."

"Maybe that's what happened."

"I'll never know. That's hard, you know? Not knowing your history or where you came from. I've thought about doing one of those mail-in DNA tests, but I'm afraid of what it might say. I might find siblings or my parents, and I don't know how I would handle that. Jack and Tiffany Hatfield were my parents."

Reaching over, I take her hand in mine. I don't have words to help her with this. She's right. There is a good chance she will never know her birth parents. "They loved you."

"They chose me," she says, the sadness evident in her tone. She stares out the window, lost in thought, and I give her the time she needs. "You know what I wish?"

I glance over at her. "What's that?"

"That they could have met you. They would have loved you for me."

I feel a weight on my chest. It's so heavy that I glance in my rearview mirror and signal to pull to the side of the road. Putting the truck in Park, I hit the button for my flashers, check the mirror one more time, and climb out of the truck.

My heart feels like it could explode out of my chest. If I didn't know that the beautiful woman in my truck was the reason, I might think I was ready to have a heart attack.

When I reach for the door handle to open her door, I see that my hands are shaking. Not from anger but from how deeply I feel for her. I've held it in. She knows I care about her, but she doesn't know to what extent.

She doesn't know that my heart is hers. But she's about to.

Gripping the handle, ignoring the way my hands shake, I pull open her door. She's already got her seat belt off and turns to face me as if she's going to get out of the truck. I don't give her a chance as I step as close to her as I can. I place my hands on her thighs and move her legs to wrap around my waist. I crush her in a hug because, damn, I just need to hold her. I need to organize my thoughts, but there is nothing but chaos in my head. Her words bouncing around like a ping-pong ball.

"That they could have met you. They would have loved you for me."

"Archer?" There's uncertainty in her voice, and I know she thinks it's something she said or did, and it was, but not in a bad way.

Pulling out of our embrace, I frame her face with my hands. Her emerald eyes are filled with questions. But there is only one answer. "I love you, Scarlett." She sucks in a haggard breath at my confession. "I'm in love with you." My chest is rapidly rising with exertion because I've held these feelings in for far too long, and it's time she knows.

"Archer," she whispers my name as tears well in her eyes.

"They chose you, and so do I. No matter where life takes us, you will always be the love of my life."

"You can't know that."

"I can. I do. I have never felt this connection with anyone else. You're my once-in-a-lifetime, baby." I kiss her softly. "I know my confession doesn't change things. I know you're destined for greater things than this small town of Willow River, Georgia, but I need you to know that wherever you are, my heart is with you."

Wet eyes spill big fat tears that roll down her cheeks. I smooth them away with my thumbs. She opens her mouth to reply but quickly shuts it as more tears fall, shaking her head. She's smiling, and that smile is so full of love I don't need her words. I can see the truth written all over her face.

"I love you too," she croaks. "There have been two people in my life who ever got those words from me. You are number three."

"Baby," I whisper. I have so many people in my life that I love and tell them openly. For her to give me hers, which so few have ever received, has my heart swelling five times its size in my chest. "I love you. I love you. I love you." I shower kisses all over her face, making her giggle. Her mom died a few years ago, which means she's gone that long without hearing those three little words. I have her for five more months and vow to tell her every single day.

"I love you."

"Best date ever." I pull back and reach for her seat belt. She turns to face the front of the truck, and I lean in and buckle her back in. I kiss her quickly because she loves me, and I love her, and that's what I want to do. Carefully, I close the door and wait for a passing car to fly by us before getting back into the truck, buckling in, and pulling back on the road. I reach for her hand, and she takes it.

"I'm so excited." Scarlett bounces on the balls of her feet as we stand in line for our third and final haunted house of the night. The first two weren't too scary, much to my dismay. I was hoping my girl would need to hold on to me, but she's always charging through each house, fearless.

"This one is supposed to be the scariest of the three," I tell her. "That's what I read online."

"I'll protect you." Her smile lights up my world.

I snag an arm around her waist, tugging her close. I wrap her in a hug as my lips connect with her temple. "How about we protect each other?" I suggest. She's quiet, so I don't think she's going to answer, or maybe she didn't hear me. Until she turns in my arms and places her gloved hands on my cheeks. I peer down at her, giving her my full attention.

"It's been a long time since I felt protected, Archer Kincaid. Thank you for loving me."

Ah, shit. Emotions well in my throat. I'm not an overly emotional guy. I love my family, and they know it. I love Scarlett, and she now knows that too. I don't get choked up, but this woman, my firecracker, has managed to do just that. I swallow hard as I press my forehead against hers. "I love you."

"I love you too."

Thankfully, the line moves forward, and it's our turn. Scarlett grabs my hand and leads us through the entire thing. We get a few startle scares, but nothing too bad. By the time we're walking out, my girl is laughing and smiling.

"That mummy guy that dropped from the ceiling got me," she confesses.

"You and me both."

"Thank you for tonight. This was so much fun."

"You're welcome." It's on the tip of my tongue to tell her that we'll make it a tradition, but I catch myself before the words can slip out. She won't be here next year. Maybe I can travel to wherever she is and take her through a few. I don't know what the future holds for us. Will we find a way back to one another? I hope so. It's going to suck living the rest of my life without my heart by my side.

Scarlett just left to go home and get ready for the work week. I'm supposed to be doing the same, but I can't seem to sit still. It's been a couple of weeks since I've stopped to visit my parents outside of Sunday dinner, so I grab my keys and head out.

I don't bother knocking because Carol and Raymond Kincaid insist that no matter how old we get or how many years we live on our own, this house, their house, will always be our home. I feel a pang of sadness in my chest for Scarlett. She lost that when she had to sell her family home.

"Hello!" I call out.

"In here," Dad calls back.

"Hey, old man," I tease as I take a seat on the opposite end of the couch. "What are you into?"

"Nothing much. Just watching a little football. What about you?"

"It's been a couple of weeks since I was here. Thought I'd check in. Where's Mom?"

"She made dinner for Rush and Crosby. You just missed her."

I nod and settle back on the couch, my eyes glued to the television. Once a commercial comes on, my dad mutes the TV. "What's eating at you, son?"

"Nothing."

He gives me a pointed look. "Try again."

I sigh. "Nothing. Scarlett went home, and my house was too quiet without her. I should be doing laundry and all kinds of other shit, but instead, I couldn't sit there without her."

"You're in love with her." It's not a question, but I answer him anyway.

"I am."

"We missed our camping trip this year." He laughs to himself.

"What does our camping trip have to do with me being in love with Scarlett?"

"Between all the rain, the work schedules you boys have, and the wives that were expecting that we didn't want to leave, we didn't get to have it."

"I know that, Dad. What are you getting at?"

"That's usually when I dole out the best advice around the campfire."

"I don't need advice."

"Don't you?"

"No."

"That's why you're here, son."

"I'm here because she wasn't there."

"She still leaving?"

"Yeah." I sigh. I haven't talked to my parents about my relationship with Scarlett. They know that we're together, but they've let me proceed how I see fit. I'm thankful for their love and support. "She's a free spirit," I tell him. "She's lost her parents, they were her world, and I think settling down scares her. She's afraid to love and lose."

"She loves you." I give him a questioning look. "It's all over her face, son, just as it is yours."

"She does. That doesn't change things, though. I can't ask her to stay, Dad. I can't ask her to give up her dreams. She settled into this plan to travel and take pictures, and she's crazy talented.

That's where her heart is, her passion. I won't ask her not to pursue that because my heart bleeds for her to stay here with me. I can't go with her. How would I make a living? It's just... not the right time for us, I guess, and that tears me up inside."

"No. You can't clip her wings. You need to leave her wild. Love her for who she is. Make sure she feels that love. She'll stay wild, but she just might come back to you."

"You trying to get my hopes up, old man?"

He laughs. "No, but I know what it's like to love and be loved by a woman I would tear the world apart for. That kind of love is hard, if not impossible, to walk away from."

"You really think we can figure this out?"

"I think there's a good chance. Are you prepared to let her stay wild? To travel with her job?"

"Yes. Yes. Yes. I can handle that. I don't know why I didn't think about that."

"I don't think you should suggest it. You have to let her chase this dream of hers the way she thinks she needs to. Then if and when she comes back to you, you let her know you're there for her. That she can keep Willow River and you as her home but still chase her dreams."

"Why the hell not? It's the perfect solution."

"Because she needs to know that you support her. She needs to know that she has you in her corner. She's lost everyone close to her. She needs that support, Archer. As bad as I know you want to present this to her and beg her to stay, son, you have to let her go."

"I get it," I tell him. "I don't like it, but I get it. Her parents supported her and encouraged her to live her dreams. I think she might be doing this for them as much as she's doing it for herself."

"I'd say you're right. Show her every day what she means to you. Be open and honest with her, and when it's her time to go, you have to let her."

"Loving her is the easiest thing I've ever done, but letting her go, that's hands down going to be the hardest."

"Nothing worth having ever comes easy," he reminds me. It's something he's told us a lot growing up. "Work hard, and love harder, son. It will all iron out in the end."

"Thanks, Dad."

"Anytime, son. Now, tell me how work's going. You should be getting laid off soon, right?"

We spend the next half hour or so talking and getting caught up on life before I say goodbye, with Dad promising to tell Mom I said hi, and I'm sorry I missed her. The drive home, I process what he said, and I know he's right, but I can't help but hope we can make this work. That I can be her home, and she can come back to me. I'm not excited about going weeks without her, but I'll take weeks over a lifetime.

Willow River
Georgia

Chapter 18

SCARLETT

I WAS NERVOUS ABOUT TODAY. Christmas was never a big affair. It had always just been the three of us. That's all we'd needed.

Then when we lost Dad, it was just Mom and me, and we were okay with that. The Kincaid family is like its own small army. Nine boys, their wives, and kids, plus Ramsey, their cousin, and her family. That's a lot of people.

I was intimidated, but I wanted to be here for Archer. There was also a small part of me that wanted to see how a large, loud family did the holiday. Let me tell you, I was not disappointed.

Carol and Raymond Kincaid know how to Christmas. As soon as we walked into the house, it smelled of warm sugar cookies. I was delighted to find out it wasn't just the scent of a burning candle but a huge tray of fresh cookies sitting on the dessert table. An entire table was full of yummy treats, which I learned that the daughters-in-law and Ramsey requested they take over. I'm glad I insisted on bringing my mom's recipe for peanut butter oatmeal bars. Archer tried to tell me I didn't need to bring anything, but I refused to come empty-handed.

"How you doing over there, Scar?" Palmer asks me.

"I'm stuffed. Mrs. Kincaid, that was incredible. Thank you for having me."

"Carol, dear, we've been over this." She gives me a kind smile. "You're always welcome here." Her voice is laced with sincerity, and my heart twists in my chest. This family has a way of making a girl wish for more.

"Daddy! Is it time for presents?" Blakely asks.

"Can we let our food settle?" Declan asks her.

"No," Blakely, Maverick, and Merrick reply at once, making everyone in the room laugh.

"Come on, Blake. Let's get a good seat." Raymond stands and holds his hand out for his granddaughter.

"Go sit with the ladies. We'll be in soon," Archer says, kissing my cheek.

"What?"

"We clean. The ladies took care of cooking and dessert. We clean up."

"Really?"

"Yes, really. Now, go so we can get to the good stuff."

"I thought dinner was the good stuff."

"Presents, Firecracker."

"What if they don't like what I brought them?" I whisper.

"Baby, I told you. My brothers and I stopped buying gifts for each other once Orrin got married. We were just passing around gift cards. We buy for our parents and the kids."

"I know, but I'm not a part of the family. I'm a guest, and I needed to show my appreciation to everyone for including me. Today has been incredible, Archer."

"You are a part of this family." He lifts my hand and places it over his heart. "You're a part of me. That makes you a part of them."

"It's not that easy, Archer."

"It actually is." I hear a deep voice behind me. I turn to see Orrin standing with his hands shoved in his pockets. "He loves you. That's good enough for us."

I turn back to Archer. "You told them?" I whisper, feeling my face heat. It's not that I care that they know we're in love, but I just didn't expect them to know or to bring it up.

"He didn't have to tell us. We can see it written all over both of you," Orrin tells me.

Something happens inside me. A warmth, a sense of belonging I've missed since losing my parents, washes over me. They accept me. They accept us. I should be worried I'm so easy for them to read, but I know that when it comes to Archer and the way I feel about him, there is no hiding. I don't want to hide it.

"I'll meet you in there." Archer smiles and kisses me—a soft press of his lips against mine—and then he's following his brother into the kitchen.

Moving into the living room, I take a seat on the floor next to the bag of gifts I brought. Kennedy motions for me to sit next to her, but I'm good here. I raise my camera and smile. "I'm going to take pictures. I'll make sure you all get copies."

"I admit. It's nice having two photographers in the family," Palmer muses. "All the pressure is off me."

"Oh, great. Now I feel the pressure." I laugh, as does Palmer. It's a great way to hide the emotions of her calling me family. To be a part of this big loving group of humans would be a true gift.

As Archer promised, the guys join us not long after. I guess when there are ten of you, because Deacon, Ramsey's husband, helped out, it doesn't take long to clean up. Archer takes a seat next to me on the floor. He leans his shoulder into mine, and I smile at him.

"Daddy said I can help pass out presents." Blakely starts digging under the tree, and with some help from her mom, she distributes packages until there is nothing left under the tree, and there are piles in front of Carol, Raymond, and the parents who have kids.

"Blakely, I have more. Do you mind helping me pass them out?" I ask her.

"Oh, no, I'm good at it."

I smile at her confidence at six. She reminds me of a kid several years older.

"Thank you." I hand her each package, telling her where to take them. Once she's done, I speak up. "It's not much, but I wanted to give you all something to show you how much I appreciate you sharing your family with me today. It's been a while since I've been with any kind of family during the holidays, and well…" I swallow back my emotions. "Thank you."

Archer wraps his arms around me, and a single tear breaks free, slipping down my cheek. I quickly wipe it away. "Go ahead and open them," he tells his family.

"This wasn't necessary," Raymond speaks up. "It was our pleasure to have your company today, Scarlett. If you ever find yourself in need of people around you, holiday or not, you get back here to Willow River. We've got you."

I smile and nod, because the tears are so close to unleashing. Archer gives me another squeeze. Rushton stands and brings me Caden. I offer him a thankful smile. His wife has a similar background, and somehow Rushton knows I need a distraction.

"Thanks, brother," Archer says, his own voice sounding gravelly.

"Oh, Scarlett," Carol says. "This is— I love it. Thank you so much." She turns her frame, one of the eleven that I brought with me. In the center is a picture that I snapped of Carol and Raymond at Crosby's baby shower. There are ten outlying images in the matted frame. Each one is the boy and their families and Ramsey and her family. At the bottom, their last name is written in script in large letters, and beneath their name, it reads, *Work hard and love harder.*

"That's why you wanted our picture," Ramsey says. "This is incredible, Scarlett."

"You told me you needed practice." Kennedy points a finger at me.

"I'm sorry I lied, but I wanted it to be a surprise."

She nods and tears into their package.

"They're all the same," I tell all of them. "I started to do something different, but the love that you all share with one another… the support you provide as a family, I thought everyone might like the same one."

"They're perfect." Palmer stands. "Take Caden, Arch." Archer does as he's told, and Palmer holds her hand out to me. I place mine in hers, and she pulls me to my feet. "We love you, Scarlett. I know you're leaving, but you need to know you have a home here. If you ever lose your way or just want a place to land, it's here. In Willow River with us." She hugs me tightly, and I return her hug as tears fall freely.

Raymond said something similar earlier, and I feel their love, their support of me following my dreams, and their sincerity of always welcoming me into their home.

"Now, give me my nephew." Palmer pulls away and takes Caden from Archer.

"Hey," he calls after her.

"I have one." Deacon stands and brings baby Brynlee over. However, he hands her to me instead of Archer. "She's prettier than you. You might scare my baby girl," Deacon teases Archer.

Archer laughs it off. I know what they're doing. They're lightening the mood, and I could hug them both for it. This family truly is incredible.

We settle in as Carol and Raymond open their gifts from each of their sons, and then the parents open gifts for their little ones. Remi, Orion, and Beckham are just over a year and enjoyed the paper more than what was beneath, and Blakely handled hers all on her own. Brynlee and Caden didn't know what was going on, but they were angels in the chaos of the moment. It's one of the greatest days and will be a memory that I will take with me forever.

"Now," Archer says as we step into his house. "Are you ready for your present?"

"Is that even a real question?" I laugh. "My bag is already under the tree." I point to the bag that I brought in earlier before we left for his parents' place.

"Oh, I know what I got."

"That frame, yes, but I got you more than that."

"Where are we doing this?" he asks.

"By the tree, of course." I kiss his cheek and move to turn on the tree lights before sitting on the floor, dragging my bag over to take everything out of it.

"You have to open one first," he says, sitting on the floor next to me.

"Why do I have to go first?"

"Because ladies are always first."

"Fine. Gimme." I hold out my hand, and he digs under the tree. There are only a few presents left. "Let's do this one." He hands me a small box.

Carefully, I peel back the wrapping paper. It's a long black box with a popular jeweler's name on the front. I open the box and gasp. "Archer."

"Do you like it?"

"I love it. It's beautiful." Inside is a charm bracelet with a few charms. I immediately recognize the camera charm. Pulling the bracelet out of the box, I look over each charm. There's a camera, a fish, a ghost, and a Christmas tree. "Is that... a firecracker?"

"Yep. I had to really search to find that one. It's my favorite."

"Archer, this is incredible. Thank you so much."

"You're welcome, baby."

"Your turn." I hand him a small box. This is more of a gag gift, but I had to get it.

He tears into the package, and when he pulls it out of the box, he falls back onto the floor, laughing hysterically. "This is epic. I love it." He holds up the Popeye bobblehead but with his face on it. I found it online, and like I said, I couldn't pass it up.

"Your turn." He reaches for another package, and there is only one left under the tree, which is a big box. I have no idea what might be inside. He hands me a medium-size box.

I make quick work of the wrapping paper and pull out a new camera bag. "Archer! This is the exact one I wanted."

"I know."

"How?"

"I listen when you talk, Firecracker."

Leaning over, I kiss him before going back to the camera bag. I pull it out of the box and the protective packaging. Something red catches my attention. I turn the bag, and tears prick my eyes. The word *Firecracker* is embroidered on the strap. "Archer."

"You like it?"

"I love it."

"I thought this way, no matter where you are, I'd be with you. Or the memory of me."

"You will forever be with me no matter where I am, Archer Kincaid. I love you."

He climbs to his knees and crawls toward me, kissing me tenderly. "I love you."

"You have two more," I tell him. "One, you already know what it is." I point to the frame that he got, just like his brothers and his parents. "And then there's this one." I hand him his final gift and bite down on my bottom lip. I hope he loves it as much as I do. I know men aren't necessarily as sentimental as women, but I hope he loves it anyway.

I watch intently as he tears off the polar bear Santa wrapping paper and lifts the lid from the box. He removes the album and opens the first page.

"'This is the day I met you. It will be a day that forever changed my life.'" He reads the caption aloud. He doesn't need to show me to know it's a picture I took of him at Alyssa and Sterling's wedding.

"What is this, Scarlett?" he asks as he turns the page.

"I wanted to give you a piece of me. A piece of us. So I started printing pictures, but then I decided to annotate them, so to speak. A piece of my thoughts about the moments we shared together. Not all of them have thoughts, but most of them do."

"Scar." His voice cracks. He clears his throat and tries again. "Baby, this is... the greatest gift I've ever received. It's like a window into your heart."

"Our story," I tell him.

"Yeah, baby. Our story."

I curl up in his lap, and together we flip through the pages. He takes his time reading every single description. I read them with him, reliving each of those moments. I don't know how I'm going to leave him. It's been weighing on my mind since we confessed that we love each other. I can't give up my dreams for love, but if there was ever a man who could hold me still, it's Archer Kincaid.

"Scarlett, baby, I love this so much." He closes the album and wraps his arms around me, resting his chin on my shoulder. "I'll cherish it forever, Scar." He's quiet and then adds, "Maybe we can add more memories to it. Not just the next few months, but you know, in the future."

"I would love that, Archer." He has no idea how much I would love that. I don't know what it will look like or how we will make it happen, but if there is a will, we'll find a way.

"Okay, time for your last gift." He taps my thigh, and I move so he can grab the bigger box and slide it across the floor to me. "This is the one I'm not sure about. I think it's the right one. If not, we can take it back and get the one you wanted."

"I'm sure whatever it is, it's perfect." I tear off the wrapping paper and gasp. "Archer! No! You did not! Archer!" I say again, because I can't believe what I'm seeing. "Is this for real?" I ask as I stare at the box.

"Yeah, baby. It's real. Is it the right one?"

"Yes. I—how—Archer!"

He laughs. "I listen when you talk, Firecracker."

"This is too much." I'm staring at the box that holds a brand-new state-of-the-art SLR camera.

"It's not too much. Every time you get into your camera bag, which I know you pack like a pistol, and every time you lift your camera to take a picture, I'll be there with you. I don't want you to leave, Scarlett, but I understand, baby. I understand, and I support your dreams. I want you to chase them and maybe come back to me every now and then."

I'm openly sobbing. "I love you. I don't want to leave you, either, but I can't give up on my passion. I'm torn. My heart is breaking at the thought of leaving you."

"I'll be right here, Scarlett. Do you remember what I told you all those months ago?"

I shake my head because all I can think about right now is that I've found him. The man of my dreams, and I can't keep him. At least not him and my career as a travel photographer. I don't see how when some assignments are months at a time. Archer deserves someone to share his life with, not someone who stops in a few times a year.

"I don't care where you are in the world, if you need me, you call me. Do you understand? My love for you doesn't stop because you're chasing your dreams. We knew this was what was going to happen. We knew you were leaving, but we didn't know you'd capture my heart."

"It hurts to even think about it."

"I know, baby. But we have to talk about it. I don't want to push this under the rug. I want to know that you understand that you are my entire fucking life. I would do anything for you."

"I want to ask you to come with me. I just can't take you away from your family and your job."

"I've thought about it," he confesses. "I don't know how I would make a living if I were to follow you around the globe."

"Just the fact that you've considered leaving your family for me, Archer, you are the greatest man I've ever met."

"Always yours," he replies. "You have to go. You have to chase your dream, and if that dream ever changes, this is where you land. Here with me."

"People change over time."

"I won't stop loving you." There is so much conviction in his tone. I'd be crazy not to believe him.

"Thank you for all of my amazing gifts." I'm changing the subject, but I have to. It hurts too much to talk about this. I know he's right that we need to, but we still have time, and I want that time. I won't let my leaving rob us of that.

"You're welcome. Thank you for mine."

"Will you hold me?"

"You ready for bed?"

"Yeah."

Together we work on cleaning up our mess and stacking our presents under the tree. I want to play with my new camera, but there will be plenty of time for that. I need his arms around me more. I unplug the tree as Archer turns out the lights and leads me to his room.

Once we're in bed, he holds me tightly all night long.

I never want him to let go.

Chapter 19

ARCHER

It's Valentine's Day. It took me weeks to decide what we were going to do tonight. When I asked Scarlett, she said to surprise her. I thought about a nice restaurant, maybe even spend the night in Atlanta, or taking her to the Mexican place she loves in Harris, but both of those options required me to share my girl, and that's not going to work for me.

We are down to weeks before her contract runs out with Palmer, and I know she's been entertaining offers for jobs. She's yet to tell me if she's taken one, and although I hate to ask her because I hate thinking about her leaving, I will.

I'm not just blowing smoke up her ass. I do support her, but I also don't want her to go. My conversation with my dad a few months ago still runs through my mind. We could find a way to make it work. I keep telling her that I'm her place to land, hoping that between assignments, she can come here so that we can spend a week or weeks together before she's called out again. At this point, I feel as though I sound like a broken record, but I need her to understand that it doesn't matter how much time passes. She'll always be the love of my life.

I used to look at it as a blessing that once a Kincaid man falls, he falls hard, and for life—at least as far as I know from our family history—but it also kind of feels like a curse. It's not that I want to love someone other than Scarlett, but the idea of living life alone, wishing for her, sounds miserable. Then I think about early in our relationship, and we both decided we'd rather have this time than not to, and I still stand behind that.

Loving Scarlett has made me a better man.

So, we're staying in tonight. I can't handle having to share her time. I'm still off work. The weather has been good, so there's talk of calling us back sometime next month. I hope it's not until after Scarlett leaves. I need as much time with her as I can get.

The house smells like baked spaghetti, something I knew that I could make and not screw up. Scarlett loves chocolate cake, so I commissioned, well, asked my mom to make one for tonight. Hers are better than anything I could have bought.

There's a knock on the door, and I call out for her to come in. She doesn't have to knock. When I don't hear footsteps, I turn off the oven and move to the door to open it for her. She's spending the night with me, so maybe her hands are full. Pulling open the door, I see my love standing with a smile on her face. She's holding a flowerpot full of sticks that have mini-candy bars attached.

"What is that?" I ask, reaching to take it from her.

"Well, I was going to bring you flowers, but then decided buying flowers for a manly man such as yourself wouldn't be the best option. So, I decided to make you a sweet bouquet instead. Get it? Sweet." She grins, proud of herself.

"Get in here before you freeze to death." I step back, letting her through, taking her overnight bag from her shoulder as she passes by me.

"It smells like pasta heaven in here. Please tell me you made your baked spaghetti. I'm starving, and that sounds so good." She doesn't wait for me to answer. Instead, she kicks off her shoes and tosses her coat over the hallway chair as she pads socked feet to the kitchen to pull open the oven.

"You really do love me," she says, turning to look over her shoulder.

Her smile is radiant, and a flash of what our future could look like crashes into me like a tidal wave. What coming home to her would look like, or her coming home to me during the winter months when I'm laid off. Making her dinner, sharing our days, our lives. Babies. Fuck me, the thought of Scarlett round with our baby has my pulse spiking.

"I do love you, Scar. So much." My voice is thick, and even though she was teasing, with the images flashing through my mind, I had to tell her. I had to say the words out loud. They're real regardless, but they needed to be voiced.

"Do you love me enough to feed me?" she asks.

I chuckle. My heavy mood of what we could be if we had the chance is pushed to the back of my mind. "You know I do," I tell her. "And guess what?"

"What?" She hops up on the counter and watches me as I remove the spaghetti from the oven.

"I had my mom make us a chocolate cake for dessert."

"Oh, God," she moans. "You know I love your mom's chocolate cake."

"I know." I get to work scooping out a plate of spaghetti. I sprinkle some fresh parmesan over the top and move to step between her legs. Reaching beside me, I pull open the silverware drawer, grab a fork, and twist the tines around until I have a bite ready for her. I blow to cool it down. "Open, Firecracker."

"What are you doing?" She laughs.

"Feeding you."

"That's not what I meant." She shakes her head but opens her mouth to accept the bite I'm offering her. She covers her mouth with her hand as she chews. I take a bite for myself, giving her time to chew before offering her another bite.

"I like this," I tell her.

"Feeding me?"

I nod. "It helps that I'm nestled between your sexy thighs with your legs wrapped around me. More than that," I keep going, "I like feeling as though I'm taking care of you. I know you don't need me to," I'm quick to tell her. "I still like the way it feels."

"You take care of me in so many ways," she tells me before taking another offered mouthful. Once she's finished chewing, I kiss her before giving her another bite and taking one for myself.

I stand between her parted thighs until the heaping plate of pasta is gone. "More?"

"No. I'm stuffed." She reaches for a napkin and wipes her face.

"Drink?"

"Water."

"Sure." I place the plate in the sink to rinse it while grabbing two bottles of water. I turn off the faucet before handing Scarlett our waters and lift her off the island. "Go find us a movie. I'll clean up."

"I can help."

"Nope. I got it, baby. Just pick us a movie. We're waiting for the cake, right?"

She groans. "I can't eat another bite."

I nod. "I'll be right there." I turn back to the sink, washing the single plate and fork, and cover the baking dish with foil. Good enough. I need her in my arms. When I make it to the living room, she's standing with the remote pointed at the TV. Her half-empty bottle of water sits next to my full one. I reach for it, twisting off the cap and drinking it until it's empty. When I twist the cap back on and place the empty bottle on the table, I see her watching me.

"What?"

"That's hot."

"What's hot?"

"The way you just downed that bottle of water."

"Really?" I ask.

"So hot, Popeye."

I shake my head. "Come here." I take a seat on the couch and pull her onto my lap. Just where I want her. "What are we watching?"

"Nothing looks good." She tosses the remote to the couch, and it bounces on the cushion beside us.

"What's going on in that beautiful head of yours?"

"I signed."

My heart drops to my toes, but I manage to nod. I give myself time to process the news. "Where are you going?"

"Michigan. The city is looking for images of the great lakes. Something about tourism." She shrugs. "I've never been to Michigan, but I hear it's beautiful."

"When do you leave?" The question feels like sandpaper on my tongue.

"The second week of March."

"That's a week sooner." Sooner than I expected is what I want to say.

"Yeah, Palmer said it was fine."

"So, I have you for four more weeks."

"Four more weeks," she confirms.

I hold her tighter because all I really want to do is beg her to stay. My heart tells me that if I ask her to stay, she will. That all she needs is for me to say the words. I want her heart to stay wild, but I want her to do that here with me.

When her body starts to shake, I feel my own emotions threatening to break free. I'm holding my heart in my hands. How am I supposed to let her just walk away? Her hands grip my shirt as sobs rack her body. All I can do is hold her. I can't form words. My throat is thick with heartbreak.

Don't go.

"I love you." My voice is a haggard whisper. "I love you," I repeat, over and over again. I can't tell her enough. I need her to understand that those three words are more than just love. They represent my soul that's now linked with hers for eternity.

"One day, Scar, one day you're going to come back to me." My voice doesn't sound like my own.

"Archer...." She snuggles closer, curling up into a ball on my lap. She sits completely still for several minutes. Hell, it could be hours. Time is passing by too fast.

Four weeks.

When she finally lifts her head, her pretty green eyes are swollen and bloodshot from her tears. She raises her hands to my cheeks and studies me. I don't know what she's looking for, but she must find it. She nods. "I need you, Archer."

"You have me. All of me."

"Make love to me."

That's the first time she's ever called it that. Making love. I've thought of it a million times, but we've never referred to it as such. Tonight, we will. I'm going to take my time and show this woman what "I love you" means. I'm going to worship her.

Standing with her in my arms, I carry her down the hall to my room. I don't worry about the lights, and I locked the door when she came in earlier. I don't worry about anything but the beauty in my arms. I place her on the bed and reach over, turning on the bedside lamp. I kneel before her and reach for her leggings. "Lift for me." She does as I ask, and in one tug, I have her leggings and her panties over her hips, down her legs, and tossed across the room. "Arms up." My voice is soft, and she complies, lifting her arms in the air. Her sweater lands somewhere behind me. I can't pull my eyes from her to find out. I don't care.

All I care about is Scarlett and showing her what she means to me. Climbing to my feet, I reach behind her and unclasp her bra, tossing it too. I reach for the hem of my shirt, but her hands over mine stop me. She stands and points to the bed. I take her spot and wordlessly lift my arms in the air. She tugs off my shirt before dropping to her knees and working at the waistband of my lounge pants.

I lift my hips and help her get them off, which leaves us both fully naked. Scarlett drops to her knees, but I shake my head. "Not tonight."

"I want to." She licks her lips.

Just thinking about her luscious mouth wrapped around my cock has me hard as steel. "I can't."

"Why?"

"Because that's not how I want to come. I need to be inside you tonight."

She studies me, not saying a word. Reaching down, I place my hands under her arms and lift her onto my lap. I hug her to me.

Skin to skin.

"So soft," I murmur as I press my lips to her shoulder. When I lift my head, her eyes are brimming with tears. Sliding my hand beneath her gorgeous red locks, I cup the back of her neck and guide her lips to mine. I take my time exploring her mouth. Her tongue slides against mine in a practiced move as if she's only ever kissed me.

I want to be her last kiss.

Her hands run through my hair, and I groan when she tugs gently. Standing with her in my arms, I turn and climb onto the bed, one leg at a time, while holding her to me, supporting her. When I'm where I want us, I lower her to the mattress. Her red hair fans out across my white cotton pillowcase. The contrast between the two is vibrant and an image I'll never forget.

I'll never forget a moment I shared with her.

I settle between her thighs, bracing my weight on my hands that are flat against the mattress. Green eyes stare up at me and I swallow hard. I wish I knew the right words to say at this moment. I'm scared as hell I'm going to end up begging her to stay, and I know that's selfish of me. This is her dream, and I'm not going to stand in the way of that.

"You are the most beautiful woman I've ever met. Inside and out," I tell her, pressing a soft kiss to her lips.

"I always dreamed of a man like you, Archer Kincaid. I didn't think men like you existed. Sexy, kind, caring, and loyal to a fault. I know we did this to ourselves. We knew the outcome, and even though it hurts like hell to think about driving away from you, when I think about the possibility of never having the moments we've shared, of never having the love of a man like you, that would be a travesty."

I lift a fist and tap my chest. "Right here, Scar. That's where you're leaving a scar on my heart, but it's not one from pain. It's a scar from loving you. One I will carry with me every day for the rest of my life."

She chokes on a sob, and all I can think to do is lower my head and kiss her. I kiss her slow and deep, needing her to feel me, needing her to remember this when she's gone. With a small thrust of my hips, I slide inside her, inside my love.

196 | KAYLEE RYAN

Dropping my weight to my elbows, I wipe at her tears with my thumbs as I take my time making love to her. There's nothing hurried about the way I pull out and slowly slide back in. Her pussy is squeezing the hell out of my cock, and that's when I realize I'm bare.

"Baby—" I croak, because fuck me, I've never felt anything like this. "I-I'm bare," I say, as I start to pull away from heaven.

Her legs lock around my back. "I'm on the pill, and I want this. I want all of you."

"You have all of me."

"I do now," she says, laying her soft hand against my cheek.

"You feel like silk wrapped around my cock. Hot, wet silk," I say, kissing her again, because there is nothing in this life that I love more than all of me touching all of her, anyway that we can make that happen.

"I can feel all of you."

"Yeah?" I pull out and slowly push back in.

"It's... different."

"Two souls connecting."

"It's our love."

"Yeah," I agree. Our love. I fight the urge to close my eyes as I don't want to miss this. I don't want to miss the way she bites down on her bottom lip when I push inside her or the way her eyes, those emerald pools of desire, stare up at me.

"Th—There," she pants. "I feel so full. Why does it feel like you're bigger without anything between us?"

"Baby, you can't say things like that, or I'm going to come before you do."

"How about you come with me?" She smiles up at me.

"You ready?"

"So close." She nods.

I quicken my pace but still take long, languid strokes. My balls tighten and a familiar feeling is tingling in the base of my spine. I'm ready to let loose, and when her pussy convulses around me and my girl calls out my name, I know I need to pull out now. I try to do just that, but she wraps her arms around my neck, squeezing hard, and her legs hug me tighter.

"Baby, I need to— You have to let me go."

"Inside me, Archer."

"Scarlett." There's warning in my tone. Her words just about send me over the edge.

"Please...."

I can never say no to her. I know she's on the pill, but there's a part of me, a very large fucking part, that hopes she gets pregnant. I know that's not the right way to bring her home, but it would. I love her. She loves me, the baby, the one I can only imagine would be conceived out of love.

"Please," she says again.

I pull out and push back in and let go. For the first time in my life, I come inside a woman without anything between us. I never want there to be anything between us ever again.

Except there's about to be miles and miles between us.

Fuck me. My heart aches.

"I love you, Scarlett," I pant as I press my lips to her forehead.

Please stay.

"I love you too."

Cautiously, I roll to the side, careful not to crush her. My legs shake as I move to the bathroom to get a wet washcloth to clean her up. Once I have her taken care of, I slide beneath the covers and hold my heart in my hands as I start to count down the days until this will no longer be possible.

Chapter 20

SCARLETT

HOW IS IT POSSIBLE THAT my heart is full and cracking at the same time? When Archer told me we had plans tonight, I told him I just wanted to stay in. I craved being wrapped in his arms until the last possible second.

Just like I have the last four weeks.

He said that he promised Palmer we would stop by. I said goodbye to her on Wednesday this week. Archer goes back to work on Monday, so we've been glued to each other's side since Wednesday afternoon. I packed up all of my belongings and turned in the keys to my rental. My bags are in my car. Everything except for what I've needed the past few days. I'll pack the last few items up in the morning before I head out of town.

I didn't expect his entire family to be here. I didn't expect the "We'll Miss You, Scarlett" banner, the food, the chocolate cake, and the cards and gifts. It's all too much. It's so much that my heart is bursting with happiness and love for these incredible humans who have become a huge part of my heart.

Then there's the hurt.

It's not just Archer I'm going to miss, although he's at the very top of that list. I've become close to his entire family, and Palmer, she's the closest, bestest friend I've ever had. I know she has Ramsey and her sisters-in-law, but she's mine, and leaving her hurts almost as much as leaving Archer.

"Scarlett." I feel a hand on my arm, and I look over to see Carol Kincaid smiling softly. "How are you, dear?"

Just the kindness in her voice has tears welling in my eyes. I shake my head, and she wraps me in a hug. It's been years since I've had the embrace of my mother, and I miss her every day, but at this moment, that pain slices through me. I latch on to Carol and hug her back as if my life depends on it.

She holds me.

I hold her.

Silent tears coat my cheeks, and I'm suddenly embarrassed. I pull back. "I'm sorry."

"Sweetheart, you have nothing to be sorry for." She offers me a tissue. Just like a momma, always prepared.

"I need you to know that I love him. With everything inside of me, I love your son."

She nods. "I know you do. He loves you too."

This time it's my turn to nod. The love between us is strong, and we don't bother to hide it. "I'm going to miss everyone. Not just Archer. Thank you for always welcoming me into your home."

"You're in my son's heart. My home will always be open to you."

My chin wobbles as I fight the battle with my tears. "Thank you."

"You know they're proud of you, right?"

I turn to look at her. Not exactly sure who she's talking about. The room is full, so it's hard to tell who she's referring to. She must see the question on my face, and her eyes soften.

"Your parents, Scarlett. They would be proud of the woman that you are. They would be happy to know that you're chasing your dreams."

"You think?" I ask, barely able to get the question out.

"I know so." She looks to the side, scanning the room. "You know, as a parent, all you want is for your children to be happy. You want them to have a career where they can support themselves and their family, and you want them to fall in love and start that family. That's really all we want. We don't care what that looks like. There are no expectations. Just happiness and love."

"They would have loved him. Truly." I wipe at my cheeks. "I can see him watching the game with my dad on Sundays having a beer, and helping my mom reach something on the top shelf. I wish so badly they could have met him."

"Family is what you make it. My sister, she's... well, she's not the best parent. She stood by while her daughter was beaten down by words and eventually fists."

"Ramsey?" I ask. I've heard a little of her story.

"Yeah. That girl, she's one of us. She had a plan for her life, one that was made for her, the expectations of her parents, but it wasn't what she wanted. She came to us, and we loved her through her transition. Now—" Carol clears her throat. "—she's the happiest I've ever seen her."

"They are happy." I'm not sure where she's going with this, but Carol has always been kind to me, so I'm going with it.

"When she got here, she was a mess. She asked us what she should do with her life, and we told her she could do whatever her heart desired. She worked hard. I watched her for two years working two, sometimes three jobs because she never wanted to depend on anyone to take care of her ever again. Then she met Deacon."

"He changed her mind?"

"His love for her did."

"It's clear what she means to him."

"He looks at her the way Archer looks at you. The way my husband looks at me and the way all my sons look at their wives."

"What are you trying to say?"

"I'm saying you should chase your dreams, Scarlett. Never let fear hold you back. I'm also saying from a parent's perspective, they would want you to be happy. Whatever that looks like."

"I promised her. It was her final days, and I promised her that I would follow my passion."

Carol nods. "Passions can change, sweetheart."

"Mom, are you hogging my girl?" Archer asks, stepping up behind me and wrapping me in his arms.

202 | KAYLEE RYAN

"Oh, just a little girl talk." Carol places her hands on my cheeks. "We're heading out soon and taking some grandbabies with us. You be safe, Scarlett, and if your travels ever bring you back to Willow River, you have family here who would love to open our doors for you." She leans in, kisses my cheek, and walks away.

"What was that about?" Archer asks.

I turn in his arms, resting my hands on his chest. "She was just saying goodbye." A goodbye that has my mind spinning like a hamster on a wheel. I understand the message. I get what she's saying, and my heart thunders when I think about changing the course of my life. I have a plan, and I've always stuck to the plan. I've always kept to myself, and it's gotten me this far. However, I didn't do that here. This small town and the people in it wouldn't allow me to.

"I can't believe this is our last night together."

"Maybe I can come back to visit," I offer. It's the first time I've talked about the future other than the fact that I'm leaving. Archer has told me I can always come home to him, and so have Palmer and his brothers and pretty much the rest of his family. Carol just told me the exact same thing.

I never wanted to think about it. I thought it would hurt worse, but it actually gives my heart hope that maybe, just maybe, one day... things can maybe be different. If he's still single, I don't know how long I'll travel. I just know it was always my plan. I might be a free spirit, but I'm also a woman of my word, and I promised my mother, the woman who chose to love me, two days before she took her final breath, that I would live my life to the fullest. Chasing dreams and never settling.

I made a promise.

I intend to keep it.

No matter how much it hurts to walk away.

"Scarlett!" Jade calls out. "Get over here and dance with us." She waves me over.

"You should go."

"Our time is running out."

"We have all night, baby. They're your friends. They're going to miss you almost as much as I am."

"Almost?"

"Yeah, Firecracker. Almost." He kisses me, taking his time to taste me fully before tearing his lips from mine and nodding for me to join his sisters-in-law on the makeshift dance floor.

He smacks me on the ass, making someone whistle and call out for us to get a room as I make my way to join the ladies to shake our asses for our men.

"Group hug!" Alyssa calls out.

The ladies gather around me, and we hug each other tightly. I'm in the center of all of them, and my heart is pumping so hard, I'm worried it might cause permanent damage. My throat constricts with tears that are threatening to fall, and I'm not so sure I can keep them at bay.

"We're going to miss you," Kennedy says.

"You have to come back to see us," Ramsey tells me.

"And the babies," Jade says. "They need their aunt Scarlett to be at their birthday parties."

"You always have a job here," Palmer tells me. "A job, a place to stay, and people who love you."

"We'll take care of him," Crosby assures me.

That's what does it. Pain slices through me, and my tears fall unchecked. I never knew I could have so many people in my corner. So many that I love and who love me back.

"Hey! We want some of that love," Maverick calls out. The next thing I know, there are ten men joining us. We're huddled together, and somehow Archer works his way to the center with me. He wraps his arms around me and holds me tightly as his family, my friends, shower us with their love.

"We love you," he says, his lips next to my ear.

Full and cracked at the same time. How will my heart ever recover? One thing I know is I will never in my entire life, no matter where that takes me, feel this ever again. This overwhelming sense of love in this moment will forever stay with me. I'll never forget a single one of these amazing people wrapping me in their love.

They've given me something I never knew I needed. Acceptance, hugs, and their love.

Everything I lost when I lost my parents, I found it here. In my wildest dreams, I never would have expected this to be where I was a year after accepting a job with Palmer.

After our group hug, the party winds down. Archer says it's time for us to go, and I know that our time is dwindling fast. I want nothing more than to curl up in his arms and soak up his love and warmth before I have to live without both.

The morning sun peeks in through the slats on the blinds covering the windows. I need to get up and get moving, but I need just five more minutes. We came back last night, and Archer made slow love to me until we both fell into an exhausted yet restless sleep.

"Morning, baby."

I lift my head from his chest and offer a sad smile. "Morning."

"What time do you have to leave?"

He already knows the answer. I'm assuming he's hoping that it will change. It's not going to. I have a twelve-plus hour drive ahead of me, and that's if I don't hit traffic. I considered flying, but I knew I would need the time to cry without onlookers. I can cry alone in my car without judgment. I don't have many personal belongings, but what I do have I wanted with me.

"I need to be on the road by eight." I rented a condo in Michigan. Sight unseen, but the company I'm working for has assured me it's clean and in a safe neighborhood. It's for three months. I've done this many times before. It's what I do. However, spending a year in Willow River has me spoiled, I guess.

"I'll make you some breakfast before you go." He kisses the top of my head.

"I'm not really that hungry," I tell him.

"Scar, you have to eat."

"I will. I'll just hit a drive-thru or something. Really, I can't stomach anything right now."

"You're all packed."

"Yeah."

"I guess we should get dressed."

I hate that he's right, but I nod because I need to get moving. We're silent as we get dressed for the day, brushing our teeth side by side. I'm slower in my movements, taking note of the way he smells and the way his eyes meet mine in the mirror. The small smile and wink he gives me. He's trying to be strong for me, but I can see the pain.

It's my pain.

Once we're finished, I pack up my last few belongings. The sound of the zipper on my suitcase cuts through the air like a knife. I go to lift it off the bed, but Archer takes it.

"Let me get that." He lifts the luggage effortlessly while holding his other hand out for me. He leads me to the front door. The suitcase is dropped, and his arms grip me like a vise. His body shudders, and I choke back a sob.

"This fucking hurts," he says gruffly. "I don't know how to let go of you."

"W—We knew—" I try, but I can't seem to form the words.

"Promise me, if you find yourself in limbo, you come to me. You call me. Fuck, Firecracker, send a damn pigeon, and I'll be there."

"I promise." I nod.

"My heart is yours. It will always be yours."

"Oh, Archer." I hug him tighter because this might be the last time I ever feel his arms around me and mine around him. "I love you. More than I ever thought was possible. It's a forever thing, Popeye," I say, trying to keep my tone light.

His reply is for his arms to tighten. He's squeezing the breath from my lungs, but I don't dare tell him. It could be the last time.

"I need to go."

"I know." He releases me and reaches for my suitcase. He opens the front door, and we step out onto the porch, only to find his yard full of people.

His people.

My people.

"W-What?" I cover my mouth, tears already falling.

I hear boots on the steps and manage to make out Raymond Kincaid as he stands in front of me. "We love harder," he says with a soft smile. "My boy isn't the only one who's going to miss you." Raymond pulls us both into a hug. "No way were we letting one of us drive out of town without us here to do a proper send-off." He steps back and waves at the yard. "Go on, sweetheart."

I reach for Archer, and he takes my hand. As he nods to his dad, together, we make our way down the steps. Each of his brothers, their wives, and their kids take their turn hugging me goodbye. And then there's Carol, as she stands next to Raymond, who has his arms wrapped around her.

"We love you, Scarlett. We're proud of you, and your parents would be proud of you."

A sob breaks free, and Archer pulls me into his chest, holding me tightly. I have never felt more loved in my entire life.

I need to leave. I need to just get into my car. One foot in front of the other. This is the plan. I'm chasing my dreams. The assignment I accepted will be in all kinds of travel brochures for Michigan. It's a huge opportunity for my career.

This is what I need to do.

I take a few deep breaths and face the crowd of Kincaids. "Thank you so much." My voice cracks, but I push through. "To have you all here. Not just for me, but for him." I turn to look at Archer over my shoulder. He's standing behind me, my back to his front. He kisses my temple, and I turn back to his family. "Take care of him for me." It's not a question because I know that they will.

"I'll never forget your kindness. Thank you for one of the best years of my life." I turn to Archer. "Walk me to my car?"

"Your suitcase is already in the back," Raymond tells us.

"Thank you." I don't look at him. I can't. It's too hard. The pain is too intense. I knew this was going to hurt, but fuck, this is not what I expected. I feel like my heart is being ripped from my chest.

We reach my car, and I can't take a full breath. Archer bends down and smiles softly. "I love you, Scarlett. Be safe, baby. Let me know how the trip is going and when you get there."

I nod.

"Chase those dreams, Firecracker. Reach for the fucking stars, and grip them in your hold."

I can't control my tears as they fall, coating my cheeks. "I love you. I'll never forget you."

"I'll see you again, baby. I promise you that."

"You never break your promises."

"Never, baby." He hugs me one more time before opening my door. I climb in, and he waits for me to be strapped in before he leans in and kisses me one more time. "Safe travels, Firecracker. Stay wild." He gives me a sad smile, and I return it.

This man... the way he loves me. It's once in a lifetime.

I nod, and he closes my door. Putting my car in Reverse, I pull out of his driveway. I glance into the rearview mirror. I should have known better. Archer stands in the center of the road, his family surrounding him as they watch me drive away.

Chapter 21

ARCHER

MY HAND IS FISTED OVER my chest, right where my heart aches. The pain is not something I've ever felt, and I know the memory of this agony, this searing inferno in my chest, will stay with me forever.

I move to the street as I watch her car disappear. I know my family joined me. I can feel them rally around me. I'd expect nothing less, but right now, I can't even form the words to tell them what it means to me that they were here for me. For her.

The pain has stolen my voice.

I'm still refusing to budge a single inch, keeping my eyes on the back of her car as she drives away, taking my heart with her.

When her car finally disappears, I suck in my first full breath since she pulled out of my driveway. I manage to mutter "Thank you" as I move to the front porch.

I don't know who I am without Scarlett.

That's scary as fuck.

I glance over at my truck, and I know that I can catch up with her. I could flash my lights, get her to pull over, and beg her to stay.

"I should have asked her to stay," I say to myself.

"You did the right thing, bro." I look up to find Orrin standing next to me. "She needs to make that choice."

I nod. I know he's right. Maybe I should call her. Tell her one more time how much I love her. No, that's just going to make this harder on both of us. By the time she checks in with me in a few hours, I'll be more composed.

Closing my eyes, I focus on breathing. I expected this to be hard, but fuck, I never expected to feel like my heart was being ripped out of my chest and packed away in the back of her Subaru.

I feel a hand on my shoulder. Then another, and another, and another. I suck in a breath, trying to hold it together. When I feel arms wrap around my waist, my eyes pop open, wishing, praying it's her, but it's Ramsey. Her eyes are shimmering with tears. I don't have time to tell her I'm okay before my parents, the rest of my sisters-in-law, and my nieces and nephews all assemble around me.

A sob cracks free from my chest, the pain so intense I'm not sure I'll ever be able to breathe without feeling its presence.

"Uncle Archer?"

I swallow hard and look over at Blakely, who's in Declan's arms. "What's up, sweetheart?"

"My heart hurts."

I reach for her, take her into my arms, and bury my face in her neck. A few tears fall before I can compose myself. "It's okay," I tell her, running my hands up her back. My family moves back, giving us a little breathing room.

"Aunt Scarlett told me a secret."

Fuck me, it hurts, yet I smile when she says Aunt Scarlett. "She did?"

"Yep." Blakely nods. "She said I had to wait until she was gone to tell you."

"She's gone, Blake." I feel like I'm choking as the words fall from my lips.

"She tolded me that you were her best friend."

I huff out a laugh because I know that's the best way Scarlett could explain to Blakely how she felt about me. "She did, huh?" Blakely bobs her head.

"I tolded her that my mommy was my daddy's best friend, too, and that she should marry you. She said that if that ever happened, she'd be the happiest she's ever been." Blakely tilts her head to the side. "Why did she leave? She should have just married us."

There are a few chuckles at her suggestion.

"She's got big dreams. A job to do."

Blakely scoffs. "I guess she likes that more than arm porn."

I can't help it. I laugh. My body shakes with it, and I hug my niece. "I love you, Blakely."

"I'm very loveable. Daddy says."

"Come on, son. We're invading your place. We brought food. We're making breakfast." I nod and take one last look at the driveway where her car used to be and follow my family into the house.

Chapter 22

SCARLETT

I WIPE MY CHEEKS WITH the back of my hand while still trying to drive. My chest is heaving, and this pain... the hurt of driving away from him is too much. It's not supposed to feel like a piece of me is no longer mine.

How am I supposed to do this?

I don't want to leave. I'm not even excited about the idea of this job. It's a dream contract, but I've yet to feel that zing of excitement about it. Not once since I signed on have I felt as if I was overjoyed.

I should be overjoyed.

I'm not.

I'm crushed.

My chest has a gaping Kincaid-size hole that will never be filled. It's not just Archer. It's his family. It's this damn town. I fell in love with all of it.

A sob falls from my lips, and I realize I can't see. There's a pull-off just before the corporation sign. I pull over and put the car in Park. My forehead rests against the steering wheel, my grip so tight I feel I might not ever be able to bend them again.

I don't know if I can do this. "Mom," I cry into the silence of my car. "Oh, how I wish you were here. I need you."

I miss her so much. I cry even harder. I'm reaching for the box of tissues, and they fall to the floor. My eyes land on the glove box, and that's when I remember the letter that sits nestled inside.

Retrieving the tissues, I clean up my face and blow my nose twice before reaching into the glove box for the letter. The plain white envelope stares back at me with my mom's handwriting. We didn't know we were losing my dad, but with Mom, we knew, and she prepared.

I still remember the day she handed me a small stack of envelopes. The one I'm looking for sits on top.

Read me when you are at a crossroads in life.

My hands shake as I hold the envelope. This is definitely a crossroads. I don't know if this is what my mom had in mind for me, but I'm hoping that somewhere inside this envelope, there will be words of inspiration. Something that will get me through this. Sliding my finger beneath the seal, I pull out the letter and begin to read.

My dearest daughter,

You are my greatest accomplishment in life. You made my dreams of becoming a mother come true, and I've loved you every day. I couldn't love you more if it were my blood flowing through your veins.

I know, a little deep, but I needed to get that out of the way. If you're reading this letter, then you are in a place in your life where you have to make a hard choice. Even though I'm not there, I hope that my words can help ease the burden of your choice.

Did I ever tell you I almost didn't marry your father? It's true. He got a new job. It was in a new state, and I didn't want to leave what I knew. I was comfortable. I was also scared. I was from Nevada, as you know. We both were, but he got a new job in Idaho, and he asked me to marry him and go with him.

I wanted to go, but I was also afraid of the unknown. I was leaving everything I knew for a man I'd only been dating for six months. I loved him. I fell fast and hard, but I was still scared. As you know, your dad and I were never close to our families. We had rough childhoods, but it was still all that I knew.

I had a scholarship to the local community college. I wanted to be a teacher, but I was certain that if I gave up that scholarship, my dreams would never come true.

I was wrong, just in case you're wondering.

One night, the night before he was set to leave, he picked me up, and I was certain I was going to tell him that I couldn't go with him. Only the opposite happened. He took me on a picnic, something he knew that I loved to do. He bought all of my favorite foods, and we talked and laughed for hours.

Hours, Scarlett. It felt like mere minutes. As we lay back on the blanket and stared up at the night sky, I tried to picture what life was going to be like without him. All that I could see was sadness and missing him. I didn't want to miss him.

My dream was set. I had a goal, and I was working toward that goal. I had a plan to make a better life for myself. Only when I thought about my future, I needed your dad to be a part of it.

I took a risk. I chose your dad. We went to the justice of the peace the next morning and were married before hitting the road to Idaho. Every adult memory has that man in it. The best part is the love that we shared, that lives on through you.

I don't know what's plaguing you, my girl. However, whatever it is, think about your future. Where do you want to be in five years? Ten? Fifteen? Which road will lead you to what you want?

We've talked a lot about your photography, and I hope that you pursue that in some way. You are too talented not to share your gift with the world. My hope for you, my daughter, is that you find a man who will love you as your father loved me. When you do, give him your all. Don't let fear keep you from something amazing.

Life is just a collection of days when you can't share it with those you love. Our family was small, and I hate that I'm leaving you in this world all alone. I know that he's out there, Scarlett. When you find him, tell him I said hi. I know that if you love him, your father and I would have too.

Love hard, my daughter. That's what makes life special. Not our talents, not how much money we make, but the love we share and the memories made from that love. You are my heart, and I know that my love lives on through you. Share that love, Scarlett. Life is too short, not to.

Good luck with your decision.

Love always,
Mom

I feel her here with me. Closing my eyes, I smell her perfume. I don't know how she knew that I would need her at some point, but her words... they resonated with me. Taking a deep breath, I picture five years. Ten years. Fifteen years. My eyes pop open, and I know what I have to do. I clean up my face as best as I can and put the car in Drive. Checking my mirrors, I turn around.

I sit up straighter in my seat as I navigate to my destination. It seems to take forever when in reality, it's a handful of minutes. His front lawn and driveway are still packed with his family's vehicles. There is an open spot, the one that I vacated not even twenty minutes ago. I pull into the drive, put the car in Park, and almost forget to turn off the engine. I leave everything but the letter in the car as I stumble out and run to the front door, shoving it into my back pocket.

Shaking my hands out at my sides, I knock on the door. I fight the urge to just barge in, but I don't know if I have the privilege anymore. I lock my fingers together in front of me as I wait for someone to answer the door.

"I'll get rid of whoever it is." I hear a male voice inside just before the door is pulled open. Sterling stands before me, his mouth agape.

"I love him."

Sterling nods, the move seeming to pull him out of his stupor. "We know you do."

"Can I see him?"

"Hey, Arch, I'm going to need you for this," Sterling calls into the house. He winks at me.

"Dammit, Sterling. No. I'm not interested in what they're selling. Not today."

"I'm going to need you to come and tell them that yourself."

"Fuck." I hear Archer mutter. Three heartbeats later—yes, I counted—my man appears in the doorway. He glares at his brother, then turns his red puffy eyes to me, shoulders slacked. "I'm sorry—" He lifts his head. "Scar?"

"Hey, Popeye."

"Is everything okay?" He looks out to the driveway at my car. The door is still hanging open.

"Everything is fine." I smile up at him, and his entire demeanor relaxes.

"What's going on, baby?"

I want to close my eyes and savor the sound of him calling me baby. I want to jump into his arms and never let him go. Of course, that's why I'm here. I can't walk away.

"I forgot something."

"Oh." He clears his throat. "Come on in, and I'll help you look for it."

"I don't need to look for it. I know where I left it."

"Okay, well, do you want to come in and get it? Or tell me where it is, and I'll get it for you?"

"I'm looking at it."

"What?"

"My heart. I forgot my heart, but I'm looking at it."

"Scarlett." There is a waver of uncertainty in his voice.

I step inside and close the door behind me. I don't bother checking if anyone can hear me. I know by now the entire house is aware that I'm here, and as quiet as this place is, I know they're hanging on my every word. That's okay. I need them to hear this too.

"I was crying so hard I couldn't see. My heart was breaking, and the pain was just too much." I pause to collect my thoughts. "I didn't even make it past the corporation limit sign." I laugh. "I was sobbing and reached for my tissues that fell to the floorboard, and then I remembered that I had letters."

"Letters?" Sterling asks, taking a small step toward me.

I nod. "My mom. We knew she was dying and she wrote me letters. They were labeled for different times in my life. One stood out that said, 'Read when you are at a crossroads in life.' I thought she'd lost her mind. I was always super curious about what was inside, but I never opened it. I assumed I would know what felt like the right time."

"Did you read the letter?" Archer asks. His eyes are filled with pain and maybe even a little hope as he hangs on my every word.

"I did. It turns out my mom knew what she was doing. She told me that I brought joy to her life and told me she loved me." I wipe at my tears, but they keep falling. "She told me that her wish for me was to be happy. She said she hoped I would do something with my passion for photography, but most of all, she hoped that I found a man to love me as my dad loved her."

"You've found him." Archer's voice is steady as he takes another step toward me. "I never met them, and I'm sorry for that. I wish

I'd have had the opportunity to meet the amazing people who raised the woman I love."

"She said— Shit, can I just read it to you?"

"If that's what you want."

I nod and reach into my back pocket and pull out the letter. I skim until I get to the part I wanted to say. He can read it all later. "She wrote: *'Life is just a collection of days when you can't share it with those you love. Our family was small, and I hate that I'm leaving you in this world all alone. I know that he's out there, Scarlett. When you find him, tell him I said hi. I know that if you love him, your father and I would have too.'*" I fold the envelope back up, shoving it into my pocket.

My eyes find Archer's, and he's watching me closely. I can't read his expression. "My mom says hello."

"Baby," he whispers, and he rushes toward me, closing the short distance between us, and picks me up in a bear hug. "I love you," he says, his face buried in my neck.

"Uncle Arch is using his arm porn! Good job, Uncle Arch." Blakely calls out, and I burst out laughing.

I'm laughing so hard my body is shaking. Archer is, too, and he places my feet back on the ground, keeping me tucked close to his side. I take a minute to catch my breath and let my eyes scan over his family.

"My dream was to be a photographer. When I lost my mom, I lost my way. She and Dad were all that I had. No other family. No siblings. I was alone. I promised my mother I'd chase my dream. I decided the day I lost her that my dream would be to travel the world and take pictures. I never wanted to feel the kind of pain that I felt when I lost her ever again. I'd been successful in that until this morning." I look up at Archer.

"Leaving you was the hardest thing I've ever done, aside from burying my parents. I convinced myself that it would be better if I chased that dream, but I realized the second I pulled out of your driveway that's not my dream anymore. I wasn't excited about the job or leaving you. My heart was in tattered pieces, and I couldn't breathe. I'm sorry I put us through that, Archer." I look at his family again, emotion clogging my throat. "All of you. You've welcomed me into your homes, into your lives, and you've given me so much love and happiness that for the first time in a very long time, maybe even ever, I feel as though I belong."

"With me," Archer says, making everyone laugh. However, he's not laughing. His voice is gravelly, and the pain is still evident. The pain I caused by driving away.

"I hope that you can all accept my apology. I want to be here. I want to work in Willow River. I want to live here and be a part of your family." I stand here, wringing my hands together as I wait for Archer to decide if he can welcome me back into his life. I keep my eyes glued to his as he processes what I've just said. He swallows hard and opens his mouth but no words come out.

Panic starts to well deep inside my belly. Does he not want me?

He lifts his hand but quickly drops it, forming a fist at his side. My eyes dart back to his, and I see a storm of emotions. I mouth, "I love you," and that's when I see it. I see his resolve crumble. His shoulders fall, and he takes a step forward.

"Done." Archer pulls me into another hug. This one is just as tight, but the implication is more. He loves me, he forgives me, and we're doing this. Together. We're going to build a life. I'm going to put down some roots, and without a shadow of a doubt, I know there will never be a day that goes by that I will regret my decision.

"You're really here?" he asks, his face buried in my neck.

"I'm here. I'm yours. Forever."

"Fuck." His voice cracks, and his arms tighten to the point that breathing is difficult, but I hold on to him just as fiercely. He eventually loosens his grip but keeps me tucked in close to his side. That's fine with me. It's where I belong.

"Are you hungry?" Carol asks.

"Um, no, thank you. My belly is still a little unsettled."

"Come on, sweetheart." She holds out her hand. "You need to eat something."

I nod and place my hand in hers. There's no use in arguing, and she's right. I know she is.

"Wait!" Palmer calls out.

"What?" I stop and give her my full attention.

"This means you still work for me, right?" she asks.

The tears well again. I've cried enough today to last me a lifetime. "I would love that."

"That's great news," Brooks speaks up. "Palmer's going to need the extra help when baby number two gets here."

"Brooks!" she scolds.

"What?"

"We were waiting."

"I'm too excited."

"Congratulations." I step back as everyone offers hugs.

"Thank you. It's early, like really early. We're six weeks. I wanted to wait until we were past the first trimester."

"Two new family members." Merrick grins. "Let's eat."

Everyone files out of the entryway and back to the living room and kitchen. "Tell me I'm not dreaming," Archer says, his arm is around my waist. His grip is firm, as if he's afraid I might disappear.

"If this is a dream, I never want to wake up."

"You're here. For good. You're staying?" There is so much hope in his voice, that if he were not holding me close, I might fall to my knees to beg his forgiveness.

"I'm here for good. I'm staying. I'm also going to need to stay with you for a few days until I can find a place."

"You live here."

"What?"

"Do you really think I'm going to let you live somewhere else? If you don't like this house, we'll sell and buy or build, but it will be together."

I open my mouth to argue and find that I don't want to. I want to live here with him. I'm ready for us to start our lives together. "Okay." One word sets the rest of our life in motion. I don't know what compelled me to answer that Help Wanted ad in Willow River, Georgia, but I will thank my lucky stars each and every day that I did.

My dream of photography, my need to take a short break from traveling led me to my heart. To a man who I love with my entire being, and a family who has done nothing but treat me as one of their own. My heart is so full it feels as if it could explode outside my chest.

"Okay." He kisses me hard before leading me to the chaos of his family for breakfast.

WILLOW RIVER, GA · HOME OF THE KINCAID BROTHERS · WILLOW RIVER, GA · HOME OF THE KINCAID BROTHERS · WILLOW RIVER, GA · HOME OF THE KINCAID BROTHERS · WILLOW RIVER, GA · HOME OF THE KINCAID BROTHERS ·

Willow River
Georgia

WWW.KAYLEERYAN.COM

Epilogue

SCARLETT

IT'S BEEN A MONTH. FOUR weeks since I chose love over my dream of being a travel photographer. I've never been happier.

Sure, the job was exciting, but it would have been lonely. I wouldn't have a man who loves me to come home to or to come home to me. I wouldn't have his family, who are now my family, to support us and make memories with.

Looking back, I didn't need my mother's letter to tell me what would make me happy, but I guess I did need her to open my eyes. My eyes are wide open now. I don't want to miss a single second of the life that Archer and I are building together.

Speaking of my man, he called me a few minutes ago and said it was a great day to go fishing. "It's April," he said. "It's time to see if the fish are biting. It's been a long week, and I can't think of anything better than a night with you on Willow River."

So, here I am, packing us lunches. This time, it's the dinner I had made for us. Meatloaf, mashed potatoes, and green beans. I was never much of a cook, but I did follow Carol's recipe to a T, and the house smells delicious. Just as I'm placing the last of what I'm packing into the cooler, the front door opens.

"Honey, I'm home," Archer calls out.

"Hey." I smile as he walks my way. He kisses me swiftly. "I'm going to grab a quick shower, and we can go."

"Okay. I'm just going to take this out to the truck."

226 | KAYLEE RYAN

"Leave it. I'll carry it."

"I'm capable, Popeye," I tease.

He grins. "Fine," he calls over his shoulder.

By the time I have the cooler and my camera loaded, the garage door is opening, and Archer is packing the chairs and poles in the back of his truck, and we're on the road.

"Do you think the lighting will be as good as the last time we were here?" I ask.

"Probably. I'll take us to the same spot. What smells so good?"

"Oh, I made your mom's meatloaf for dinner."

He groans in appreciation, and I chuckle. We talk about our day, and before I know it, we're pulling into the same field as before. The wildflowers are already blooming, and my hands itch to get my camera.

We climb out of the truck, and instead of setting up our chairs, Archer surprises me when he says he wants to walk the field with me.

"Really?"

"Yeah. I want to see it from your eyes."

That's a good enough explanation for me. We walk to the rocks that I stood on last time, and he helps me stand. I'm looking out at the water. My camera is raised when he clears his throat. Looking down, I see he's on one knee.

"Archer?"

"I want to share my life with you. I want to share my family with you. I want you to take my last name." He swallows hard. "I have never felt the kind of love that I feel for you, Scarlett. I never want a day to pass that our love isn't solidified in every single way." He reaches into his pocket and pulls out a small black box. "Will you marry me, Firecracker?"

I'm nodding yes before I can say the words. He stays on one knee, holding the ring out, and I force the words past my lips. "Yes. Yes, I'll marry you." He stands, plucks the ring from the box, drops the box to the ground, and slides the ring onto my finger. "I love you."

"I love you too."

"Hell yeah!" I turn to see Brooks and Palmer walking toward us.

"What are they doing here?"

"I needed photographic evidence."

"That would be me." Palmer raises her camera and gives it a little shake.

"Welcome to the family, Scarlett. Not that you weren't already a part of us," Brooks tells me.

"Thank you." Hot tears prick my eyes. Some days it's hard for me to believe this is my life. I have the love of the best man I know, and his family is now my family. It's everything I ever could have hoped for and more. The fact that he had Palmer here to capture this moment is everything. I never want to forget this day and the love that fills my heart.

Archer lifts me off the rock and kisses me soundly before Brooks and Palmer take turns hugging me. Archer pulls me back into his arms as we thank his brother and sister-in-law for coming. Once they're headed back to their truck, he leads me back to his. He grips my hips, lifting me onto the tailgate. "I want you to know that I never want you to change. I want you to stay wild, just like this field of flowers."

"You think you can handle me for a lifetime?" I ask.

"Eternity, baby."

Epilogue

ARCHER

I'M GETTING MARRIED TODAY. I'VE been waiting on this day since the moment I proposed, but there was a lot going on.

Blakely turned seven. We had Memorial Day, then Remi turned two, and then last week it was the Fourth of July. We didn't want to take away from any of those days, and we didn't want to get married on a holiday.

So here we are. We're getting married at the park side of Willow River. It's where I proposed, and Scarlett said all the trees and the river would be the perfect backdrop for pictures. I didn't care where we got married, as long as it was soon.

I can't wait for her to be Scarlett Kincaid.

Something that I'd hoped for but wasn't sure would ever happen, and the day is finally here. We have three tents set up. One for the groom, one for the bride, and one huge ten that will be for the wedding and the reception. Once we settled on a date, the women in my family rallied to give my girl her dream wedding.

I'm currently standing in a tent all on my own. Orrin brought me a letter from Scarlett, and everyone left to give me some privacy to read it. I stare down at the white envelope and run my thumb across the writing. This letter isn't from my bride. It's from her mother. I'm running out of time because I know any minute, one of my brothers is going to stick his head inside this tent and tell me it's go time. The envelope reads: *To the man who marries my daughter.* Smiling, I slide my finger beneath the seal. I pull the letter out and start to read.

To my son-in-law,

If you're reading this, I approve. You see, my daughter, she's always been strong-willed. It's going to take a strong man to love her wild spirit. It's also not hard to like you when I know that we have something in common.

We both chose to love her.

Being her mother was the greatest gift of my life. I want that for her. To have a family who loves and supports her. Your family will be all she has.

Thank you for loving my girl. For not giving up when I know she fought not to let you into her heart. It's a wonderful place to be once she lets you in. My time with her was way too short, but the impact that she made on my life will live on through you, through her, and your children and grandchildren.

Be happy. Never go to bed angry, and if you do anything, please let her stay wild. She's got a big heart, and she loves big, too, but you already know that. Make sure she sticks with her photography in some manner. She loves it. I hope you already know that, but if not, help her find that again.

Congratulations, son, and welcome to the family.

Love,
Tiffany
A.K.A.: Your mother-in-law

"Thank you, Tiffany. I promise to always love her." I shove the letter back into its envelope when Ryder steps into the tent.

"Hey, man, you ready to do this thing?"

"I was born ready." I turn to face him as he's pulling his phone out of his pocket. He reads the message as I take one last look in the mirror. "Let's do this." I turn back to him, and he's standing still, staring at his phone. "Ryder?"

He looks up and shoves his phone back into his pocket. "Sorry."

"What's going on?"

"Nothing."

"Ryder."

"Jordyn's back."

The words hit me like a punch to the gut, so I know it's knocked him on his ass. I open my mouth to say something, but I'm not sure what to say. Did he know she was coming home? I have so many questions, but my soon-to-be bride is waiting for me.

"Let's get you married, and we can figure out my love life after, yeah?" He plasters on a fake smile, and I have no choice but to let him.

"I've got you, brother," I say, tugging him into a hug.

"Thanks, man. Let's go get you a wife."

Thank YOU

for taking the time to read *Stay Wild*.

Want more from the Kincaid Brothers?
Look for Ryder's story, ***Stay Present***,
releases January 23, 2024. Grab your copy here
kayleeryan.com/books/stay-present

Never miss a new release:
Newsletter Sign-up
Be the first to hear about free content, new releases, cover
reveals, sales, and more. kayleeryan.com/subscribe/

Discover more about Kaylee's books here
kayleeryan.com

Did you know that Orrin Kincaid has his own story?
Grab ***Stay Always*** for free here
kayleeryan.com/books/stay-always/

Start the Riggins Brothers Series for FREE.
Download ***Play by Play*** now
kayleeryan.com/books/play-by-play/

More from KAYLEE RYAN

With You Series:
Anywhere with You | More with You | Everything with You

Soul Serenade Series:
Emphatic | Assured | Definite | Insistent

Southern Heart Series:
Southern Pleasure | Southern Desire
Southern Attraction | Southern Devotion

Unexpected Arrivals Series
Unexpected Reality |Unexpected Fight | Unexpected Fall
Unexpected Bond | Unexpected Odds

Riggins Brothers Series:
Play by Play | Layer by Layer | Piece by Piece
Kiss by Kiss | Touch by Touch | Beat by Beat

Entangled Hearts Duet:
Agony | Bliss

Cocky Hero Club:
Lucky Bastard

Mason Creek Series:
Perfect Embrace

More from KAYLEE RYAN

Standalone Titles:
Tempting Tatum | Unwrapping Tatum | Levitate
Just Say When | I Just Want You | Reminding Avery

Hey, Whiskey | Pull You Through | Remedy | The Difference
Trust the Push | Forever After All
Misconception | Never with Me

Out of Reach Series:
Beyond the Bases | Beyond the Game
Beyond the Play | Beyond the Team

Co-written with Lacey Black:

Fair Lakes Series:
It's Not Over | Just Getting Started | Can't Fight It

Standalone Titles:
Boy Trouble | Home to You | Beneath the Fallen Stars

Co-writing as Rebel Shaw with Lacey Black:
Royal | Crying Shame

Acknowledgments

To my readers:

This story took me on an emotional journey. I didn't mean for it to be that way, but I cried like a baby while writing it. Thank you for sticking with me through the pain of their journey. Speaking of journeys, thank you for taking this one with me.

To my family:

I love you. You hold me up and support me every day. I can't imagine my life without you as my support system. Thank you for believing in me and being there to celebrate my success.

Sara Eirew:

I've been holding onto this one for a while. Thank you for another great image.

Tami Integrity Formatting:

Thank you for making Stay Wild beautiful. You're amazing, and I cannot thank you enough for all that you do.

Book Cover Boutique:

You nailed this series. I rambled about what I wanted, and you came up with something even better. Thank you!

My beta team:

Jamie, Stacy, Lauren, Erica, and Franci, I would be lost without you. You read my words as much as I do, and I can't tell you what your input and all the time you give means to me. With countless messages and bouncing ideas, you ladies keep me sane with the characters are being anything but. Thank you from the bottom of my heart for taking this wild ride with me.

My ARC team:

An amazing group of readers who shout about my books from the rooftops, and I couldn't be more grateful for every single one of you. Thank you for being a part of the team and a critical part of every single release.

Give Me Books:

With every release, your team works diligently to get my book in the hands of bloggers. I cannot tell you how thankful I am for your services.

Grey's Promotions:

Thank you for your support with this release. I am so grateful for your team.

Deaton Author Services, Editing 4 Indies, Jo Thompson, & Jess Hodge:

Thank you for giving this book a fresh set of eyes. I appreciate each of you helping me make this book the best that it can be.

Becky Johnson:

I could not do this without you. Thank you for pushing me and making me work for it.

Chasidy Renee:

How did I survive without you? Thank you for making my life so much easier.

Lacey Black:

There isn't much I can say that I have not already, except for I love ya, girl. Your friendship means the world to me. Thank you for being you.

Bloggers:

Thank you doesn't seem like enough. You don't get paid to do what you do. It's from the kindness of your heart and your love of reading that fuels you. Without you, without your pages, your voice, your reviews, spreading the word it would be so much harder, if not impossible, to get my words in reader's hands. I can't tell you how much your never-ending support means to me. Thank you for being you, thank you for all that you do.

To my reader group, Kaylee's Crew:

You are my people. I love chatting with you. I'm honored to have you on this journey with me. Thank you for reading, sharing, commenting, suggesting, the teasers, the messages all of it. Thank you from the bottom of my heart for all that you do. Your support is everything!

Much love,

Kaylee Ryan
AUTHOR